As ever, to Sarah
and to Jennifer, Julie, and Ian
and to Lynn Nesbit and Deanne Urmy

THE
EASTERN
SHORE

Ward Just

Mariner Books
Houghton Mifflin Harcourt
BOSTON   NEW YORK

First Mariner Books edition 2017

hmhco.com

Library of Congress Cataloging-in-Publication Data
Names: Just, Ward S., author
Title: The Eastern Shore / Ward Just.
Description: Boston : Houghton Mifflin Harcourt, 2016.
Identifiers: LCCN 2016002947 (print) | LCCN 2016007013 (ebook)
ISBN 9780544836587 (hardcover) | ISBN 9780544836617 (ebook)
ISBN 9781328745576 (pbk.)
Subjects: LCSH: Newspaper editors — Fiction. | Life change events — Fiction. |
BISAC: FICTION / General. | FICTION / Political.
Classification: LCC PS3560.U75 E23 2016 (print) | LCC PS3560.U75 (ebook)
DDC 813/.54 — dc23
LC record available at http://lccn.loc.gov/2016002947

Printed in the United States of America
DOC 10 9 8 7 6 5 4 3 2 1

ALSO BY WARD JUST

NOVELS

A Soldier of the Revolution 1970
Stringer 1974
Nicholson at Large 1975
A Family Trust 1978
In the City of Fear 1982
The American Blues 1984
The American Ambassador 1987
Jack Gance 1989
The Translator 1991
Ambition & Love 1994
Echo House 1997
A Dangerous Friend 1999
The Weather in Berlin 2002
An Unfinished Season 2004
Forgetfulness 2006
Exiles in the Garden 2009
Rodin's Debutante 2011
American Romantic 2014

SHORT STORIES

The Congressman Who Loved Flaubert 1973
Honor, Power, Riches, Fame, and the Love of Women 1979
Twenty-one: Selected Stories 1990
(reissued in 1998 as *The Congressman Who
Loved Flaubert: 21 Stories and Novellas*)

NONFICTION

To What End 1968
Military Men 1970

PLAY

Lowell Limpett 2001

THE EASTERN SHORE

One

UNCLE RALPH

UNCLE RALPH LIVED in the nursing home on the southern side of town, a solitary building on a low hill, low-slung, horizontal. It was built in 1912, the architect a disciple of Frank Lloyd Wright, the cost raised by subscription and a modest rise in property taxes. Everyone agreed it was a fine facility. The staff consisted of one doctor and three capable nurses, more than adequate to care for the twenty-two residents, ten men and twelve women, all but one in their seventies and eighties. Uncle Ralph was fifty-two. He occupied a small room on the second floor with a distant view of the Daggett River and the nine-hole golf course beyond. Everett Nursing Home was run loosely. Family and friends could visit anytime they wanted between ten a.m. and eight p.m. Two of the men and four women were senile and did not leave their rooms. Uncle Ralph was known as the Sergeant because he was a veteran of the Great War, a survivor of the Western Front. His memory was phenomenal, story after story tumbling from it in a husky baritone. Everyone knew that among his many wounds was a slice of shrapnel to the throat. Uncle Ralph was fond of standing at the window of his room and remarking that the golf course's sand traps reminded him of the craters left by artillery bombardments in the war, except the craters were much deeper, eight, ten feet in places, whereas the sand traps were shallow. Also, there were fewer sand traps than craters. Still, when he looked at the sand traps he thought of bomb craters. The foursomes on the golf course reminded him of infantry. Nine irons became Mausers, and billed caps the heavy iron helmets of the German army.

Uncle Ralph's Saturday-afternoon audience was his nephew Ned Ayres, little Neddy, a bright and inquisitive boy who never seemed to tire of his uncle's war stories. Listen carefully, Uncle Ralph would say in his husky voice. This was July 1918. We were closing on Ludendorff's forty divisions. We moved out at dawn from Meaux and marched east to Trilport. From Trilport to Changis and Favant and Nogen and Charly and, at last, Château-Thierry. They were just little French villages, some of them deserted or mostly deserted. The weather was warm and our boots kicked up a storm of dust from the roads, French dust. We don't have dust like that here in Indiana. The dust was frightful. Choking dust. You could suffocate from it and when the dust got bad enough you put on your gas mask. You were unable to get away from it, damned dust. In your hair and eyes and your boots and your—and here Uncle Ralph glanced at Neddy, pausing fractionally—crotch. It was in your ears and under your fingernails. It blotted out the sky, you see, and that was a good thing because the Hun air force was about, deadly bastards. God, they were vicious. Later that day we had a soft rain that put down the dust even though it remained in your pockets and eyelids. Never seen anything like it here in Indiana. I don't know how they managed to live there day by day, the French peasant class. Filthy stuff, dust.

Ugh, Neddy said, glancing furtively at his uncle, whose voice had risen as if he were on a parade ground. Uncle Ralph was shaped like a barrel, short of stature, entirely bald with scars here and there on his head and arms. He wore thick-lensed wire spectacles and heavy workman's shoes. His hands were dainty, unlike the rest of him. His light blue eyes were mere slits behind the spectacles and his eyelids. Now he coughed twice, a kind of lumbar whistle.

Château-Thierry was the objective. The front line. Beyond it was Ludendorff in person. The crown prince—*Kronprinz*—was there somewhere too. Forty divisions spread over a hundred miles, a killing ground all right. Uncle Ralph paused there, collecting himself, his eyes half shut as if he were struggling for something, a name or a face, some fugitive emotion or buried memory. And then he smiled. Rubbed his hands together and leaned close to Neddy. He said, This is confidential. Between us. I'm going to tell you a secret, the way things were back then.

We saw the Hun from a distance. They came from the forest into twilight. Wolves were among them, mangy creatures, undisciplined, furtive in the shadows. And then the wolves vanished and the German infantry was in our midst. They were big men, most of them bearded. They had had a bad time of it, you could see that. They were weary. And they carried gifts, candy bars and chocolate bears, bunches of flowers. They looked half starved but they couldn't've been friendlier. Some of them spoke English. Only a few were armed, their Mausers slung over their shoulders, barrels down. Up close they were not fearsome. They were playful as children, these German boys, asking questions and not always waiting for answers. Why, they stayed with us an hour or more. Of course we had come to a halt. The light rain continued to fall as the sky darkened. We were still miles from Château-Thierry but no one seemed to mind. They began slowly to drift away, our

German enemy. They disappeared into the rain one by one. The colonel commanding removed his shako and gave us a friendly wave. *Auf Wiedersehen.* He was a fine-looking officer, at ease on his horse. Darkness continued to fall until at last there was only us Americans. Our expeditionary force. We were alone. The ground around us was littered with candy wrappers and flower petals. You know, Neddy, there's goodness in everyone. The goodness must be sought out and accepted when you find it. Often it's buried deep, depending on the situation, the time of day and so forth. The challenge. So, we set off with light hearts. Our morale was good. We marched on and didn't reach Château-Thierry until well after midnight. Gosh, we were bushed. We'd had it by then, don't you see. At dawn the guns began to fire and we marched off in the direction of the guns.

Uncle Ralph stopped there and lit a cigarette, his fingers trembling.

At a sudden noise behind him, Neddy turned. His father was in the doorway.

Hi Neddy, hi Ralph.

Eric, Ralph said.

I've heard the most wonderful story, Neddy said.

You're lucky, his father said. Your Uncle Ralph has a million of them.

I'm tired, Ralph said.

No wonder, Eric said.

What do you mean by that?

It's tiring, telling stories, don't you think?

I suppose, Ralph said.

Eric Ayres looked at his watch. Is there anything you need?

I want to take a nap, Ralph said.

Well, Eric said. Next Saturday, then.

Neddy was on his feet, his hand on his uncle's shoulder. Ralph did not respond, his eyes half shut once again. Neddy knew he was in another place, not here, somewhere private. He knew from past experience that his uncle would not speak again. He looked up at his father, so lean and tall. It was hard to believe he was Ralph's brother. Hard to believe they were members of the same family, born only five years apart but Ralph looked years older. Ralph, seated, was bunched up like a fist, his only movement the hand that held his cigarette, back and forth from his mouth to the ashtray on the floor. Neddy was reminded of a musician's metronome. No one spoke in the gathering silence, something unresolved. Neddy understood that it was up to him to put things right.

Bye, Uncle Ralph. Thanks for the story.

So long, Ralph, his father said.

Ralph Ayres nodded. Neddy thought he saw a smile or the beginnings of a smile, anyhow something forgiving. Uncle Ralph was a fine man. He had been everywhere, in the war and later on. He was experienced. He had seen the German army up close, and other things in Europe and America. He had even been to the West Coast, lived there for a time until his ill health intervened and he returned home to Indiana and the Everett, where he was so well liked because of his kindly disposition.

Neddy and his father were quiet during the ride home. Then Neddy told him of the dust of French roads and the unexpected meeting with the German soldiers, the candy bars and chocolate bears and the rest. Flowers. The sound of artillery, the long march to—and he could not remember the name of the French city.

Château-Thierry, his father said.

Yes, that's the one. The objective.

His father cleared his throat. He said, I've mentioned this before. You mustn't take Ralph's stories to heart. That's all they are, stories.

I know, Neddy said.

But you don't believe me, his father said.

I do. But I love them all the same.

I mean, the stories are not true.

But they're wonderful, Neddy said. The German army. The French dust. The chocolate bears and candy bars.

Neddy, how old are you?

Eight going on nine.

Old enough to know the difference.

But Uncle Ralph was there. He saw it.

He saw something, all right. But they weren't candy bars.

How do you know? Were you there?

No, Eric Ayres said. I wasn't there. And I don't care for that tone of voice.

I'm sorry.

It's all right.

Neddy turned to look out the window at the nursing home receding far behind them. The dying sun cast a light that set the windows ablaze. For a moment the boy was reminded of the German artillery. He watched the nursing home disappear as they turned onto Benjamin Franklin Boulevard. He looked at his father, relaxed behind the wheel of his Buick.

Why would Uncle Ralph tell a story that wasn't true?

Well, he believes it.

He believes something that's not true?

He's made it up in his mind, son. To him his stories are true, as if his war happened yesterday. He's never gotten free of it. Ralph does not live in present time. When Neddy looked at him doubtfully, his father tried to explain. I think I've used the wrong word, son. Uncle Ralph's stories are not *factual*.

Huh, Neddy said.

That's cleared it up for you, right? His father was smiling.

Do you like Uncle Ralph?

Certainly I do. He's my brother.

I love Uncle Ralph, the boy said.

Eric Ayres was silent a moment, thinking of his brother, five years older, broken in mind and spirit. A hand grenade had seen to that. From time to time he had to be restrained, administered tranquilizers, watched around the clock. Saturday was always his best day. Nothing could be done about Ralph. Neddy's visits meant everything to him. Eric wished his boy was not quite so understanding. Eric Ayres released a long sigh. He was a circuit judge known for his probity on the bench. With the probity came a certain acerbity. His dry wit was especially helpful. He despised sloppy preparation, meaning windy arguments. The only levity in his courtroom was his own, the dry wit. Eric Ayres was a deacon in the Presbyterian church and valued rectitude. He believed in facts. He believed in a stern God and saw himself as a fireman directing his hose at the mendacious and the ignorant, the ten-percenters and their hangers-on. The illusionists.

Can I go next Saturday?

Of course you can, his father said.

I want to bring Uncle Ralph a present.

What a good idea. We'll go to Grant's, buy him a necktie. How's that?

That's good, Neddy said. And I can listen to the stories?

7

Most of all listen to the stories.

It's all right, then?

Yes, it's all right.

I don't have to believe them, Neddy said.

Believe them if you want to, his father said. But remember, they are not factual.

Two

JOKE TOWN

T HE NEIGHBORHOOD WAS ordinary enough, houses of brick, houses of stucco, a few houses of stone, one house of clapboard built in the previous century and now derelict, an eyesore. Across Grove Street from the Ayreses' place was a park with a baseball diamond and two tennis courts bounded by a concrete curb. When winter came the courts were flooded to make an ice-skating rink. Grove Street was shadowed by giant chestnut trees, the sidewalk littered with shiny chestnuts. The iceman in his one-horse wagon came on Thursdays, the mailman twice a day, every day except Saturday. The Wednesday mail brought *Life* magazine with its photographs of the outside world, the Alhambra, a grizzly bear in Alaska, the Sphinx, a sidewalk café on the Champs-Élysées in Paris, France, everyone smiling for the camera. La Belle France free, liberated at last. Of course these places were out of reach, photographs in a magazine, life elsewhere. They might have been on Mars—and by the way, there was also a brilliant photograph of the crowded galaxy, Mars in there somewhere, theoretically. Supposedly. And how could you know for certain? There were many galaxies and this could be the wrong one. Young Ned Ayres asked the iceman about it but the iceman didn't know.

I deliver ice, kid. Ask your old man. And when young Ned did, his father pointed at the shelf containing *The World Book Encyclopedia* and said, Look it up. But the encyclopedia was no help in deciphering the photograph in *Life* magazine. Probably in New York City they would know the answer. His father often referred to New York as a city filled with know-it-alls. The mysteries of the galaxies would have to wait awhile. It seemed to Ned that everything outside the town was a mystery.

The town was called Herman, situated in Indiana, cut from plain cloth, some farming of soybeans and corn, a pencil factory at the spur of the rail line, silos beyond. The Daggett River cut through the center of town, then meandered away, diminishing as it approached the Ohio, well downstate. A peaceable town, anyone would agree, with the usual rural amenities. A stone pile on Benjamin Franklin Boulevard with a neon sign in the front window: Elks Club. Two gas stations, one at the north end of town, the other at the south. Winters were snowy and the days unnaturally short, but summer afternoons seemed to go on forever, the air soft as a hummingbird's trill, a breeze so light you could hold it in your fingers. Such a fine climate, even considering the tornadoes that touched down, did their work, and passed on. The tornado was the price paid for the sublime summer afternoons, when things moved at a half trot. One day was much like the next, and the years—they, too, had a sameness, sledding and ice-skating in the winter, golf and baseball in the summer. A mile or so out of town to the south stood the nine-hole Daggett Golf Club, its fairways flat as pool tables but with surprising sand traps and thick stands of towering oaks and chestnut trees and of course the slow-moving river that ran—strolled, rather—diagonally through the third, sixth, and ninth fairways. The Daggett was the center of social life in Herman, the annual New Year's Eve party a particular occasion, business suits for the men, gowns for the women, paper hats, balloons, and a six-piece band from the high school. They played well, too. There was a raffle on New Year's Eve to benefit the nursing home. Ned's father, the circuit judge, was the longtime president of the club.

Like so many small communities near and far, Herman was badly bruised by the Great Depression, not that anyone from outside—that was the phrase for strangers, those from outside—gave much notice. Why would they? Herman was isolated, and when anyone asked for its exact location they were told, Not so far from Muncie. Herman began to thrive again during the Second World War, the pencil factory running three shifts a day, the farmers selling anything they could grow. The town reached its apex of prosperity in the late 1950s, and then it commenced a long, slow decline. The population of the town grew older as young people moved away, many of them to the assembly lines of Detroit. The pencil factory was sold, and sold again, and finally shut its doors. Marshall's department store was next to go, followed by the Buick dealership. Kresge's five-and-dime went away and William Grant Haberdashery—well, the less said about that, the better. The Congregational church across the street from the courthouse burned to the ground, with arson suspected but never proved, and in what seemed no time at all Benjamin Franklin Boulevard was a ghost zone. Most poignant to Ned was the early retirement of Mrs. Lindsay, the piano teacher. It seemed to him, on his frequent visits home, that an entire culture was in ruins—and Herman was a fine place to grow up in, its parks and stately trees and the slow-flowing Daggett giving a kind of civic reassurance. The schools were good. Crime was negligible. People looked after their neighbors. If you were able to accommodate yourself to listless rhythms, you could build a decent life in Herman and hand that life down to your children and grandchildren.

But the distance between listless and exhausted was short, and when Ned learned that the weekly newspaper had failed, its mighty Goss presses sold for scrap—well, that closed the door. Ned had grown up on the *Press-Gazette*, from summer reporter to managing editor, all before he was twenty years old, when he ran away to the morning paper in cosmopolitan Indianapolis. The struggle with his father was titanic. First, Ned had refused to enroll in college; next, he proposed a career in journalism. Judge Ayres was enraged; he had seen newspaper reporters go about their work and was not impressed. They were downside men. He thought them cynical, and the cynicism was unearned. Reporting was a convenient way of avoiding civic responsibility. Much more convenient to write about a problem than actually devise a solution. They led disheveled personal lives. The judge called them cavemen, preferring to write about shadows on the wall than what was in front of their own eyes. They were hell-raisers and drinkers, and the idea that his son, so bright, such a nice boy, would choose that business was—appalling, and worst of all his wife, Olive, saw nothing wrong with it.

She said, Let Neddy chart his own course.

He's off course, that's the problem!

He'll be fine, Olive said.

It's a junk business, Eric insisted.

Not to him it isn't, Olive said.

What the hell's gotten into him?

The world has gotten into him, Eric.

Not to go to college. Not even to try. Bright as he is. It's disgraceful.

You're not listening. He doesn't want the classroom. He wants the street.

You call that ambition?

It's what he wants, Eric. And if I were you, I'd make it up to him. Or you'll find yourself on the outside.

I'm not on the outside. He is.

Neddy was a prodigy and a dedicated inside man, an editor, soft-spoken and polite, easy to get along with, somewhat shy, a façade that concealed a fierce ambition. Herman did not reward the strongly ambitious—getting a little ahead of yourself, aren't you, son?—so Ned learned to keep that side of himself private. However, he was a demanding editor. As his reporters said, The best blue pencil in the business.

In due course, Ned's father died and his mother relocated to the Everett Nursing Home, in fact down the corridor and around the corner from Uncle Ralph's old room. She had a nice view of cornfields and the low rise of a hill and in the evening she could watch the sun set. Ralph had died the year before his brother. Ned never failed to say a prayer when he was visiting his mother after wishing the sergeant Godspeed. His mother's mind had gone to pieces. She was unable to recognize her only child, and indeed rarely spoke when Ned visited. The Everett was failing also, the plumbing erratic and the air conditioning long since switched off. By all rights the Everett should have been condemned as unsafe but there was no place to put the residents. The town had no budget for the necessary repairs so the Everett limped on. Ned's visits to his mother were brief, and he contented himself by remembering who she had been and what she looked like when he was a boy, her good humor and teasing. Olive Ayres had been an astute observer of Herman, having grown up in Bloomington, where her father was a professor at the university who specialized in the mores of rural life. He had written a book on the subject, *Dead Reckoning*, a title Eric Ayres despised for its sarcasm and condescension. When they were alone, Eric told his son to pay no attention to his grandfather, who had been born in Massachusetts. Fancy pants, Eric called him. Bolshevik. Olive listened carefully to her father's theories, nailing the fly to the wall as it were. Ned often heard her tease his father. He heard her say one night, Herman's such a *moral* little town, adding a playful giggle. So different from Bloomington, its night life and other amusements, including some hanky-panky. Do you realize, she said, that we know only one divorced couple? We know everyone in town, for God sakes. Plus which, half the people we know don't even have children. What is it? Something in the water? Ned's father replied patiently, Herman's quiet, always has been. No one liked broken crockery. People want to sin, they go to Chicago. Maybe St. Louis. Or a barn somewhere.

Olive said, There's no sin in Herman?

Oh, his father replied, the usual. Nothing much beyond that.

So they go to Chicago. What do they do there?

Rent a hotel room, I suppose.

I imagine they'd go in separate cars.

I imagine they would, Olive.

With some alibi, a story. A cover story.

I'm sure an alibi would be involved.

I'd better never catch you with an alibi.

And the judge laughed and laughed, and then, because the evening was young, he said, How about a game of gin rummy, Ollie?

A small town, then, like so many in Middle America with an absence of commotion. Herman was what it was, neither more nor less. However, the town did have one singular distinction. It was known from coast to coast because it was the hometown of one of the most popular comedians of the day, Ed Watts, a fixture on Sunday-night radio and later on television. The comedian's signature routine was a monologue involving Herman. He pronounced it Herrrrrrman and everyone laughed. Then he would tell a story about Herrrrrrman, its narrow-mindedness, its tedium, its squeaky-clean government, its tubby cheerleaders and bone-dumb policemen, its boiling summers and frigid winters when everyone skated on the frozen waters of the shallow Daggett or the Grove Street tennis courts. As if Herman were in Holland! There was malice in his tone, getting even for—well, it could be anything, such as an unproductive and unhappy childhood. Girls loathed him and boys baited him, or that was the supposition, because strangely enough very few in town remembered Ed Watts, his looks or his bearing or where he lived or what his father did. Was he the skinny kid who threw spitballs in math class? Maybe. Maybe not. Just about every small town in America had a local hero, someone who had gone away to the wider world and made good. But instead of a baseball player or minor movie star or musician, Herman had Ed Watts, nonentity, who now lived in a twenty-room mansion in Beverly Hills with five Persian cats and busy wife number four, quite a step up from the three-room bungalow at the wrong end of Benjamin Franklin Boulevard. That was the burden of the cover story in *Collier's*, headlined "From Herman to Hollywood: The Ed Watts Story."

Of course Ed Watts was as popular in Herman as he was elsewhere in America, even as the adults squirmed in discomfort. Their wised-up children laughed, somehow in on the joke and flattered that their town was as well known as South Bend or Muncie. For the adults Ed Watts was a mixed blessing, amusing as an entertainer known from coast to coast, perhaps not so amusing in other

15

contexts. This was the ordeal for any resident of Herman: checking into a hotel in Detroit or renting a car in Chicago, presenting a driver's license, the traveler would be forced to confirm the obvious: yes, he lived in *that* Herman. And the clerk would grin and say Herrrrrrman and expect a grin in return because the drawl was so funny. More often than not the clerk would turn to a colleague and say, Here's a guy from Herrrrrrman! Can you believe it? And the guy from Herman would leave the desk feeling ever so slightly diminished, his identity—well, not stolen, but disclosed. The comedian was beloved, more or less, and after his death people all over America remembered Herrrrrrman and the clowns who lived there. Ed Watts made particular sport of the Christmas pageant, the parade, and the sing-along that followed it. Men on stilts, women dressed as Mother Hubbard, the children as elves. The broadcast was an Ed Watts classic, repeated annually at holiday time. As Herman continued its long decline, those who remained saw an outrageous violation of the proprieties, of privacy itself, a cheap slander. In its own fashion, Herman was a forgiving town, good-natured and slow to take offense. But the slander was not forgotten.

Ned Ayres witnessed all this from a position of neutrality. Perhaps better said, a position of on the one hand this and on the other hand that. Ed Watts did strike a chord, however discordant. Ned knew there was some Herman inside himself, the reticence, the reluctance to judge harshly, suppressed appreciation of the yahoo antics of the town fathers, including his own father. The town seemed to Ned frozen in a past where time did not move except to regress. Ambition was frowned upon. The modern world did not intrude. At eight or so every night, homework completed, Ned slipped out the back door of his house to the big chestnut in the backyard for a clandestine cigarette. He crouched at the base of the tree and looked to the heavens where the uncountable stars spun in their orbits. Years before, his Uncle Ralph had given him a pair of field binoculars and he trained those at the sky, the stars now coming into focus but still without form. He thought of each star harboring a society of its own, with its special surroundings and civilization, its own language and religion. Somewhere high up was a young man very like himself, trying and not succeeding to understand the known world. His earth, too, was motionless while all around it the mysterious stars and planets whirled, each with its specific destination. Ned lit another cigarette and reprised his day, an interminable math class, something incomprehensible in Algebra Two. Ned watched a star fall and disappear. Doris Day was featured at the movie house downtown. Their neighbor had bought a Volkswagen, now the subject of great curiosity. A German car, the only one in Herman. It might as well have been from Mars. Ned attempted a smoke ring and failed. God, he wanted something else, but he did not know what that something else was. He refused to live and die in Herman. He believed he was looking at a stone wall. An article in the paper that afternoon disclosed that Herman's population was in the upper five percent of longevity in the state of Indiana. He tried to imagine himself at sixty-five in Herman. He would be editor of the newspaper. He would have 2.5 children. He would not own a Volkswagen. He would marry a beautiful young girl who would in a few years be no longer beautiful or young. He himself would run to fat and failing eyesight. He put the binoculars to his eyes once again and was surprised to see a winking red light, an aircraft from somewhere. He had never seen an aircraft in the Herman sky except for the occasional crop-duster. This aircraft was flying west to east. He knew what he wanted. He didn't know how to get there. He wanted out.

• • •

Later on, Ned Ayres came to believe that Herman's citizens grew up with a foreordained inferiority complex, an unnatural modesty that derived from a kind of existential embarrassment, a deformity like a hunchback or a stammer. Herman was not alone; there were hundreds of Hermans in America. But Ned's Herman felt trapped in a world of Ed Watts's making, going slowly to seed, an object of derision. Ned's father the judge thought it was nonsense. Be at ease, Eric Ayres advised. It's only a joke. Forget it. Ignore it. It's only Ed Watts, for God sakes, a third-rate vaudevillian going rapidly out of fashion himself. But Herman's morale was low and sinking, and the truth was this: anonymous at home, the town was notorious abroad. The inhabitants had trouble enough getting on from day to day with their children leaving home and the stores and businesses closing, the town growing old, a gray-haired community without aspiration. The word for it was morbid. No one saw a way up or a way out, either. They believed they were trapped inside a comedian's cliché. Herman. Their joke town.

Many years later, in Chicago for a conference, Ned decided to pay Herman a visit. He supposed it would be his last. He booked a rental car—no jokes this time from the young woman behind the desk, but of course Ned's driver's license was issued in the District of Columbia. He took the thruway south, then turned east on a two-lane highway that would take him near Muncie on the way to Herman. It was a fine day in late October, autumn slowly dissolving into winter. The fields of grain were fading in the pale sunlight. The farther south he drove, the more pickup trucks he encountered. All the trucks seemed to have a rifle athwart the rear window. Yet the terrain was peaceable and the traffic light. He felt conspicuous in his red Chevrolet. The NPR station began to fade, then was lost altogether. The land was flat, then became hilly as he pressed south. He passed one small town after another, the towns

remarkably similar, most of them announced by high church stee-
ples or farmers' silos. All the towns were sleepy in the twilight.
And all this time he was thinking of Herman and his boyhood, Sat-
urdays with Uncle Ralph, evenings under the chestnut tree with a
pack of Lucky Strikes and the bright stars above. Without noticing
what he was doing Ned had slowed his pace from seventy miles an
hour to forty. He knew he was bringing some disdain to what was
in front of his eyes. He had escaped the rural life, the quiet regu-
larity of the seasons. His life had commenced in Herman but it
would not end there. Bad luck, bad cards, Herman was a failure of
the imagination. Ned's decision to leave Herman had caused a rift
with his father that was never healed. His mother was more sympathetic, but still she was in tears when he announced his decision to leave home for Indianapolis and a job as copyeditor on the
paper there, one hundred dollars a week, a living wage then. His
father was enraged, his only son throwing his life into an ashcan.
What's wrong, Herman not good enough for you? He went on in
that manner, his voice rising until Ned was tired of listening. He
said at last, rather grandly he thought, I'm trying to escape history,
you, Herman, my assigned seat at the table . . .

His father hit him then and he went down, stars in his eyes and
his mother's awful moan in his ears, loud enough for the neighbors
to hear. Her hands flew to her mouth. When his father reached
down to help him up, Ned swatted the hand away, rose under his
own power, and left the room to pack quietly and leave the house
by the back door. He was gone before they knew it, and a year
lapsed before they were reconciled as a family, everyone giving a
little, more than they wanted to, except Ned's mother, who had
watched things go out of control in that chaotic moment but was
unable to referee. Her son was as stubborn as she was. And he
wanted another sort of life in a place that, whatever and wherever

it was, was not Herman. She had seen this coming and dreaded it. She had feared losing him to the outside world. Well, he had the stamina for it. He certainly was old beyond his years and he wanted it badly, whatever "it" was, beyond his desire to be quits with Herman.

Ned remembered all that now, shaking his head at the melodrama of it. "Escape history." Where had that come from? He had no idea. The phrase had come to mind and he used it, as anyone would. He remembered stopping by the nursing home to say goodbye to Uncle Ralph, but he was not available, "a bad day." So Ned left Herman without saying goodbye to anyone. He drove on at low speed. Suddenly the road and its surroundings became familiar. He reckoned Herman was fifty miles distant. He passed a political billboard—*Lindahl's the One! Lindahl for Senate!* The election was only a few days away. Herman had always been Republican and the billboard displayed dancing elephants in the corners. Ned wondered if Lindahl was little Jerry Lindahl from grade school, a doctor's son who wore brown wool knickers and was taunted for it. Jerry Lindahl would be an unlikely candidate even without the Herman albatross. Ned had never encountered a classmate in all the years he had been away, Indianapolis and Chicago and finally Washington. It seemed that no one ever left Herman, or if they did, they stayed in the landlocked heartland. He remembered other classmates from the period. He'd had a crush on a girl, Roberta—Bobby—a pretty brunette. They shared a desire to get away from Herman, Ned to pursue his dream of editing a newspaper, Bobby to become a nurse in a large municipal hospital, one equipped with all the latest gear. Ned said she could do much better than that. Why not a doctor? Of course she was offended. Why wouldn't she be? Both Ned and Bobby were thought to be old for their ages, Ned's plans centering on one of the Chicago papers. Yes, he thought, she was a hell of a nice girl, bright and focused; and then her family moved to Terre Haute and they lost touch. His mother told him that Bobby had taken a nursing job at the Mill City hospital, a few miles down the road from Herman. She was a nurse in obstetrics or oncology, one of those two. Mill City was a town of roughnecks, many of whom found themselves in Judge Ayres's courtroom. Breaking and entering. Assault and battery. Drunken driving. The usual plea was nolo contendere.

Then Ned saw Herman in the distance, and a moment after that the sand traps of the Daggett Golf Club. Off to the right, on the low rise on the outside of town, he saw what looked like the shell of the Everett Nursing Home, where his mother and Uncle Ralph had died. From that distance the home appeared to be unoccupied. Ned continued to drive up Benjamin Franklin Boulevard. The *Press-Gazette* property was now a parking lot, half filled in midafternoon. Across the street was a bodega. There were coffee shops and a tavern whose name was unfamiliar to him. The courthouse was unchanged, a four-story Victorian pile with dormers and a flagpole out front. When his father died so suddenly, the Herman bar wanted to name the building the Eric E. Ayres Courthouse, but nothing came of it. Ned turned at Grove Street and motored slowly to the house he grew up in, the brick one at the corner of Elm. It looked the same. Children's toys lay scattered in the front yard. If Ned expected an epiphany he was disappointed. He stopped at the curb and got out of the car, wondering about the smell. There was always a special aroma composed of chestnut and oak. It was there still. The sidewalks and lawns were covered with leaves.

Ned had come to Herman to say a word at his father's and mother's and Uncle Ralph's graves, but now he had trouble remembering exactly where the cemetery was. This was strange. He was having a memory block, everything slightly out of kilter. He thought he had made a mistake coming here. Everyone in his family was dead. The town looked shabby, and what he had to go by was the aroma of fallen leaves. His red Chevrolet was the only splash of color in the neighborhood. Ned was an intruder. He did not belong here. He remembered then that the cemetery was near the nursing home, not within sight of it but close by. Other memories came to him but they were featureless. They did not signify. How long had it been since he had seen Herman? Twenty years anyhow, his mother's funeral, the entire town turned out, at least that portion of it over forty years old. A few of his contemporaries attended, approached to shake hands, offered a pleasantry—You haven't changed a bit, Neddy—and backed away. He put the car in gear and returned to Benjamin Franklin Boulevard, made a right, and in a few moments he was motoring up the one-lane road. The cemetery was situated in a shallow depression surrounded by a cyclone fence in disrepair, the same cyclone fence that was there in his boyhood, the gate always open, no lock. Ned stopped the car and looked at the cemetery while he listened to the *tic-tic* of the car's engine. He was alone, no one in sight.

Ned had not eaten lunch and his stomach was hollow. He lit a cigarette and stood leaning against the fence gate. The cemetery was untended. Most of the gravestones were atilt in the soft earth. They were gravestones made of marble or granite. He remembered that the stonecutter lived in Mill City. He had the reputation of a fine craftsman. There were a few monuments five or six feet tall, the banker's family and lawyers and the surgeon. The haberdasher. They were mostly clustered in one section, along with his father and mother and Uncle Ralph. Off to the rear many of the gravestones dated from the nineteenth century. Two tornadoes in April of 1876 killed a score of residents and injured many more. The tornadoes came out of nowhere, sudden as a cloudburst. Black April they called it. The graves were overgrown with weeds and thickets of bramble. Crushed cigarette butts were scattered here and there, some of them of recent vintage. Bottles and beer cans were part of the litter. So this was where the boys and girls of Herman assembled at night, as they had done for decades. Ned remembered it well. Probably if he looked hard enough he could find a used condom or two or three. Rare in his day, not so rare now. However, he had no particular desire to scavenge used condoms.

He found the three graves of his family without difficulty. They looked a century old and without ornament of any kind, only the names and dates and a decayed flowerpot. The names and dates were still legible. Ned said silent prayers for his parents and for Uncle Ralph, different prayers but with a common blessing. Godspeed. He gathered a few loose rocks and placed them atop the gravestones. Now that he was here, he was glad he had come. He expressed hope that these dead were together and content. Ralph with his war stories, his mother's teasing, his father's laugh, and then he remembered their quarrels. The judge was quarrelsome, and only his Ollie could tame him when his moods ran amok. At dinner on election night, 1960, she announced that she had voted for the Irishman. Oh, my God, Eric Ayres said. You couldn't've. Not that! That wretched father, bootlegger and skirt chaser, tried to buy the election—

Ollie stood up and said, a little jump to her voice, I voted for him because he is beautiful! And the other one isn't.

Ned bent to brush twigs off the gravestones, then noticed the cobwebs at the base. He moved them aside with the toe of his shoe, scattering the long-legged spiders, filthy insects. He crushed a few and ground them into the dirt. He thought there was something precarious about the gravestones and the mostly forgotten souls beneath the earth. His father had bought a plot for him, too, without saying anything about it. The only mention of it was in the old man's will. So somewhere in the vicinity was his own resting place, an eternity of Uncle Ralph's war stories, his father's certitudes, and his mother's merry laugh. But Ned had the idea he would buy space in Rock Creek Park, perhaps invite some friends to join him when the time came. At least Rock Creek Park was well tended. There would always be the possibility that some stranger would happen by and remark, Ned Ayres, wasn't he the editor of the paper? My goodness, he had a long life! Ned laughed out loud at that. At the far corner of this cemetery was a shack for tools, but the shack looked derelict. Ned pulled at the brambles surrounding the three graves but they would not yield, stiff as barbed wire. Ned Ayres stood quietly a moment, wondering how the cemetery could be allowed to deteriorate in this way. He reached to collect a few of the cigarette packs and empty bottles. He put them aside. It was criminal, really, the disorder. No doubt the reason was that Herman was broke.

Ned stood at the graves a long while. He knew this was the last time he would visit. Herman was so out of the way. He backed off and checked his wristwatch, late afternoon, rain in the air. Dusk was coming in a rush. His stomach growled and he thought of dinner somewhere, a drink and a fat sirloin. He wondered where he would spend the night. Not Herman. There were no hotels in Herman. Neither did he wish a meal at the taberna, an addition since his time. He supposed there was an immigrant community, refugees from Mexico or Puerto Rico. Good luck to them. Probably to the immigrants Herman was a paradise: the taberna, a school system, houses selling for a song. The rule of law, more or less. He wondered if, when the immigrants began to die, someone would take charge of the cemetery. In the meantime there was a decent hotel in Muncie and good restaurants and only an hour or so away. Ned turned his back to the graves and walked out of the cemetery, hurrying now, saying one more silent prayer that surely would be heard by someone.

He paused on the way out of town, pulling off the road in order to look again at the nursing home high on its hill, gradually disappearing piece by piece in the gathering darkness. In that aqueous light the Everett had the aspect of a prison long abandoned, lifeless, diminishing as he looked at it. Why had he come here? There was nothing for him in Herman. Herman represented past time and Ned Ayres had always looked to the future, tomorrow's newspaper, the promise of things. But—this was the future, wasn't it? This wasn't yesterday. It was tomorrow. His throat filled up. Shadows embraced the Everett until it was lost to view.

Three

ELAINE

THE DREAM ARRIVED fully formed at two a.m. on a Sunday morning. He knew the time because the little clock in his living room chimed softly twice. He was in a familiar neighborhood, either Herman or Indianapolis. Ned was standing on the sidewalk of a residential street, massive houses with outsized windows and enormous oaks in the front yards. There were pedestrians, too, also outsized, giants almost, even the women. They moved cautiously to and fro as if they had no fixed destination. They were not threatening but not benign either. Ned decided at once that what he saw was more hallucination than dream. He watched events unfold behind his eyelids, as on a movie screen. He was awake in a world of his own making. The sky was purplish. Heavy clouds gathered above the hills back of the houses and soon it was raining, heavy drops the size of marbles. They rolled off the pavement and into the gutter, causing a racket, the rustling of linen bedsheets. He understood suddenly that this was a Chicago neighborhood not far from his office. The rain ceased. The pedestrians vanished, all but a lone figure in a double-breasted blue serge suit who raised his hand in a gesture of farewell. Then he disappeared, leaving Ned alone on the sidewalk of the unfamiliar neighborhood for which he was somehow responsible. Ned was fully awake now and frightened. He felt himself imprisoned in the bed. On the corner ahead was a newsboy delivering papers, and then he, too, vanished. Beside Ned, someone stirred and murmured something incoherent but evidently an endearment. Whoa, he thought. Whoa. He was unable to open his eyes. The rain turned to drizzle.

Extra! the newsboy called from somewhere out of sight. Extra!

The woman beside him said, Shhh.

The clock chimed once again, three times.

Then Ned was asleep and dreaming, though the next morning he could not recount the dream. He tried and tried with no success. He knew it was nothing like the hallucination, which was easy to recall, each frame of the film. He wrote it down later on, one for the archives. Still, it made no sense to him, and when he tried to tell Elaine, it made no sense to her. Forget it, she said. But he had already written it down. Something so strange was worth keeping. Perhaps there was an omen in it somewhere, a key to the future.

Whyever would you want a key to the future? Elaine said.

He said, Maybe I have no choice.

You always have a choice, Elaine said. What nonsense.

Later that morning they took a walk along the lake. The day was mild. A breeze had come up from the west, ruffling the lake waters. They were each preoccupied with their own thoughts, Ned Ayres with his midnight hallucination, Elaine Ardmore with her doubts about Ned. Now and again Ned would make an observation, an ore boat far out on the horizon, probably bound for Gary. A sentence, then he was quiet. Elaine was not certain she could make a life with this Ned, who had recently informed her that he had

had a cot installed in his office at the paper, the better to supervise his staff, unruly at all times. Every few days there was a late-night story, a gangbang or a fire. Fires were common, except for the one last Thursday that had killed fifteen children and the three nuns who were in charge. His staff had mishandled the story and in the confusion no one had notified the managing editor. That was Ned. He was determined to set things right on day two and days three, four, and five. Elaine did not see him for a week. He seemed to her obsessed with news, bringing to it a passion that properly belonged elsewhere. Her own self, for example. A hurried telephone call from an exhausted Ned. Distant, preoccupied. At such a time Elaine was not even second fiddle. She was a near-anonymous musician in the back row of the orchestra. With him, she had decided, it was more than ambition. It was a kind of lust, a days-long preoccupation. He was fascinated by the thing itself, news. As for his hallucination, any numbskull could figure that out. The man in the double-breasted blue suit was Dad, an admonishment. The judge doing what he did best, making a ruling. Adjudicating. Judging. Elaine sighed. It was so darned transparent. Ned's life was transparent generally, even the hallucinations, which made it visible if not entirely comprehensible. He did love her and told her so. She believed him. He was faithful to her and considerate—when he was not sleeping on his cot in the newsroom, chasing commas. Better commas than the interns. He did seem to have no other life outside the newsroom, its news and intrigues, its relentless—one might say remorseless—competition with the other papers in town. She went with him to the Christmas party and he was good with her, introducing her to the other editors and reporters, the publisher. Everyone was drinking and most of them were frankly drunk, hilarious in the fluorescent glow of the newsroom, the interns, too. Everyone was polite, but in their manner Elaine saw that she was an outsider and would always be an outsider. Could you make a marriage with one an insider and the other an outsider? Since Ned would always have another life?

And she herself was adrift so far as employment was concerned. More than anything she wanted to travel, Europe first, then Asia. In school she excelled in geography and botany, but where did that lead? She did not wish to teach. She did wish to see the Alps and the Mekong Delta, Surabaya and Cape Town. When she described these places to Ned, he looked at her blankly. Most men did. How did you earn a living in Surabaya? It was awkward for her to explain that she had money, via a salty grandmother, recently deceased. Elaine was Gamma's favorite. Gamma left her a trust that would take her around the world nine times if that was what she wanted. Spend the money, El. Let it sit and it'll begin to rot like tomatoes. The trouble with American girls is that they don't know geography and have no desire to learn. You will be different. You will travel the known world and that will lead you to the unknown world where you will meet a fabulous gentleman of means. Perhaps slightly older, a man of the world without bad habits. A man who holds his liquor. These days, you only find them abroad. Be careful of your virginity, El. You can lose it. But make sure it's a good moment to do so. You will have a life I never had. Do take my advice. It's hard-won, El. Elaine was much tempted, wondering now if Ned would be there when she returned. Of course he would. Where else would he go? But after seeing the world, would she want to return to Chicago? And if she did, would she want Ned Ayres? Elaine looked sideways at him, so lost in thought. His mouth was moving, talking to himself again. He made no sound. His eyes were narrowed, squinting. He took her hand, pausing

29

a moment to inspect the boats in the inner harbor, rocking gently in the breeze. The lake was vacant, odd because the day was fine. Elaine wondered why none of the boats were out and about. And then she saw a small cabin cruiser slip its mooring and motor slowly to the mouth of the harbor. Elaine saw Ned steal a look at his wristwatch. His stealth irritated her.

Ned watched the boat and its helmsman head to open water.

He said, Maybe we should take up a sport together. Tennis, golf.

She said, What about daggers?

Fencing? We could do fencing. It's dangerous, though.

And when would we have time for that, given your busy, busy schedule?

They walked on. The cabin cruiser gathered speed, turning to starboard, heading east and soon lost to view. Ahead of them were sharp reports, shotgun rounds from the skeet shooters at the Lincoln Park Gun Club. They were shooting doubles, *bang-bang*. Ned reminded her that the gun club champion was a woman. They could see her now, beautifully turned out in khaki trousers and vest, black boots, a man's fedora, chamois gloves, and Ray-Bans with amber lenses. One of the men said something to her and she laughed, but not before she had scored another double, *bang-bang*.

Elaine said, Maybe that's our sport, shotguns at fifty paces.

Ned did not reply, listening instead to the siren of a police prowler. He thought to himself that it sounded like a skirmish, the siren and the shotgun reports. He had an idea that Sports should do something on the gun club and the woman champion. The sports pages lacked women. He made a mental note to talk to the sports editor, who would disapprove but was attentive to Ned's suggestions. Instruction was more like it.

He said, Can we turn around? I have to get back to the office.

On a beautiful Saturday afternoon, Elaine said.

Yes, but after Saturday comes Sunday, and that's the big paper, right? Fat with news. Our bestseller.

Right, she said.

The one that pays the rent. Sunday.

You bet, she said.

He glanced at his watch again and said, Sorry.

Do you know the woman in the amber glasses?

I've met her once or twice.

Is she fun?

I guess so. I guess she's fun. She's a hell of a good shot.

Well, that would make the difference.

Come on, Elaine, let's go back.

I'll be leaving tomorrow, she said.

Where are you going? This is sudden.

I'm going to visit my father.

Your father's in Italy.

True enough. I haven't seen him in ages.

But we have plans for Sunday night. You've forgotten —

I haven't forgotten.

— the symphony.

The symphony will be there when I return.

And when will that be?

Who knows, Ned. It's pretty much open-ended as things stand now.

He opened his mouth to say something more, then didn't. He was damned if he was going to plead with her. Instead, he shook his head and looked at his watch.

Will you stop looking at the time. Just stop it.

I'm late.

Catch a cab.

I'll see you at home, he said.

Or not, she said.

Or not, he agreed.

A combustible conversation, anyone would agree. It did seem to Ned Ayres that it came from nowhere. Probably it began with his crack about paying the rent. She disliked talking about money, a matter of upbringing. It was normal for her to trash the symphony tickets and fly to Capri where her father lived. Then his pride became involved. She seemed to want him on bended knee, and that wasn't the way things worked. He would not ask her for permission. She seemed to be asking him to choose between her and his work. She wasn't beautiful when she was mad, either, her mouth a thin line and her eyes hard as marbles. At another time he might have turned her head with a joke, but not this time. He thought that at some level Elaine did not understand his work or even know what it was, the craft of editing. What it meant to be in charge, the way readers depended on a reliable newspaper, a product you could trust. It wasn't a Holy Grail or the Nobel Peace Prize and the occasional blunder was built into the job. So the editor cited the blunder, apologized for it, and got on with the job. Ned had fallen for her in part because she knew nothing of his work. His shop talk stopped at the office, pretty much. Occasionally he would call her attention to a particularly smart piece of work. She would read it with apparent pleasure, then set it aside without comment and return to whatever she was doing. He was not certain she valued what he did. She preferred the radio, the music and the talk.

This time he was only reminding her that he had to go to the office, as working people did in order to earn a living. It seemed that Capri had trumped Anton Bruckner. The nasty little secret was that just then he preferred the office company to her company.

He and El had been walking for an hour or more, had looked at the boats, had watched the gunners at skeet. His place was downtown; the Sunday paper required his supervision. He knew that she did not understand that fully. And so she made a row and decided to play her trump in order to close things off. Assert her independence, if that was what it was. Probably it was that. Really it was a sullen little power struggle that she did not intend to lose. She was lovely, though, easygoing, with an enchanting smile and a ready wit. A creative bedmate also. Often in the night she would ease herself from bed and tiptoe to the window seat, recline, and watch the empty street. She moved like a dancer, careful to make no sound. A single streetlight threw a gaunt glow as if from a forty-watt bulb. She lay motionless, appreciating the after-midnight stillness and intermittent intrusions, a clumsy couple walking arm in arm, voices loud in the street. Elaine would raise her head in a little frown, then lie back. In a moment she would be humming something, a popular song. She sang in the shower and when she was driving. He thought she knew when he was watching her and when he was asleep. If the night was warm she removed her negligee and lay nude, her hands on her belly. He thought of her posture as self-possession. On the window seat Elaine was utterly herself, an object of desire no less than a brilliant dawn rising over a windless blue sea. In time she returned to bed, lying close, wondering if he would like an encore.

But there was this one thing that they seemed unable to avoid, and maybe she had a point that there was something spoiled about the news business. The newsroom had a nearly fifty percent divorce rate. Hard drinking was the norm, and not only the staff but the spouses of the staff. During the past year Ned had wondered again and again if he would remain a bachelor for the rest of his days. He was happy enough with his own company and the com-

33

pany of his colleagues so long as a girlfriend was part of the ensemble. No question that Elaine had made his apartment livable, curtains and so forth, a serviceable kitchen, a fine kilim on the living room floor, and a tiny Miró in the bedroom. Gamma's compliments.

Thus brooding, Ned returned to the newsroom, which, as it happened, was in full-blown crisis of the sort that put a smile on everyone's face. An alderman had been caught in bed with a woman not his wife. Her husband discovered them and beat the alderman to death. What made the story most interesting was the spotless reputation of the alderman, well educated, hard-working, much admired. Ned did not arrive home until midnight, opening the door and calling for Elaine and finding only silence. She was gone. Her wardrobe was gone. She left no note.

Ned poured himself a large whiskey and sat on the window seat. He wondered what it was that fascinated El so about an empty street at midnight. Then his mind wandered back to the alderman, one of life's puzzles. He was a daily communicant at Our Lady of Sorrows on the South Side, a mild-mannered, almost meek politician who had been an accountant before entering what he called public service. He was a little under five feet six inches, wire-rimmed eyeglasses, a little potbelly somewhat out of place in a man barely thirty-five years old. He had a reedy voice that seemed to belong in a choir. He rarely spoke during the tumultuous debates that took place in the City Council, and when he was noticed at all he appeared frightened. Yet the resulting legislation often bore his mark. He was a master of ambiguity, often helpful in writing a tax law or a revision of the zoning code. As it turned out, he was a favorite of City Hall. And at the funeral, with his wife and children gathered around his casket, a high shriek was heard from the fourth pew—his paramour near overcome with grief. To complete the confusion, his name was Kurtz. Ned himself did the extensive editing of the piece, an hour-long chore that tried to reconcile the anomalies and succeeded, mostly. Still, with all his skill Ned Ayres was unable to reach the pith of the matter, its essence. He was obliged to tread most lightly on the presence of the paramour, a handsome redheaded woman, age twenty-five, long-legged, shapely, daughter of a prominent lawyer, friend of the publisher of the newspaper.

It was often remarked that men and women in the newspaper trade became cynical early, adopting a side-of-the-mouth sarcasm owing to the base metals of what they called news, a mind-numbing hurly-burly of corrupt politicians and vicious gangsters, arsonists and sexual predators and all the rest. The cat in the tree. An infant lost and found. Their cynicism was honestly acquired but had little to do with the hurly-burly. It had to do with the milieu of continual surprise. Just when you thought you had a handle on the story something utterly strange presented itself. Something off-key. Out of sync, a person, place, or thing that did not belong. The reporter sought coherence, but there was no coherence. Instead there was whirl. Whirl ruled. And the facts fell willy-nilly from an overburdened tree, yet habitually a few facts short. As for the newsroom cynicism, it was also true that the worst thing a reporter could be called was naïve. A parasol in a pigsty.

So Elaine flew off to Capri and Rome and was silent for half a year. Then a postcard arrived, dateline Cape Town, written in her tiny script. The weather was clear, the city beautiful. She had arranged a safari with friends. At last she would see a rhino in the wild. They were traveling with a white hunter who promised elephants and Cape buffalo as well. They were a jolly crew, two British and a Frenchwoman and a languid Italian. Her father had been in good form; even the wife, Tre, was agreeable. Rome was gorgeous, the monuments and artworks spectacular, the food good. I bought you a Borsalino hat. She signed off, Love, E. Ned Ayres stood at the window of his apartment wondering where Cape Town fit into her scheme of things. He was in the dark. She seemed to be a wanderer, a vagabond, his polar opposite. The fact was, they were not on the same page.

Elaine receded in Ned Ayres's thoughts, arriving occasionally in the evening hours. He concluded that he and Elaine were competitors as well as lovers, more alike than he thought, same pea, different pods. Or the other way around. Maybe what they were, were good friends. Ned lived in the present moment and Elaine Ardmore did not. The news business was a present-day effort with a nod to the past. The future was tomorrow's paper. That was Ned's context day to day. He feared that Elaine had no context because she did not work. The working life was a mystery to her, an interference instead of a context. A few weeks into their romance he discovered that she did not read his paper or any paper. At first he was offended, then amused. How could anyone live without the news? El spoke often of travel, going somewhere, anywhere that was, as she said, not-here. He never quite got the point of it, not-here as a destination. Not-here would soon enough become here, another here, and wouldn't that require a reordering of things, a life of endless not-heres, the last stop always just out of reach?

Ned's incapacity to get the point, a consequence of Herman. The incapacity was a legacy of Herman and there was damn-all he could do about it even if he wanted to. Ned had slipped with ease from Herman and Indianapolis to Chicago, but that was a matter of the job, where the work was. He could settle anywhere, St. Louis or Milwaukee, if that was where the job was. For the moment Ned Ayres was exactly where he wanted to be. You stayed in one place until you mastered it, and he supposed the opposite was true of El. She saw the world as her homeland or, to be accurate, her potential homeland, because so far she had rarely ventured from Chicago. And now she was in Cape Town, South Africa. He hoped they would meet again, in friendship if nothing else. Then he laughed out loud. Their nation could not exist half slave and half free.

Months later he received a cable at his apartment. The circumstances were forever in his memory. He was doodling on a notepad, trying to conceive a fresh means of covering the presidential election. Mahler's Second Symphony was on the phonograph, a mighty inspiration. He wondered if campaign coverage could resemble a symphony, violins carrying the melody, a warning from the horns, provocation from the big bass drum. The melody now light, now grave. A presentation not excluding humor. All the relevant facts, but the facts made clear. Given context. Given verification. Made readable. He drew sets of intersecting lines as he listened to Mahler's horns, warning signals. Ned looked up, irritated by the knock at his door.

Darling Neddy, the cable began. You must join me at once. You have no idea of the strangeness of life here, how vivid, how exotic. My heart beats to it. It's a world apart and beyond fascinating. More like fabulous. The beasts of the field on a rampage, kin to tiny earthquakes. Strange birds float overhead, a rhino as big as a tank thunders by and the eland take no notice. Life untamed, Neddy. We think we are the rulers here because we are armed and the beasts are not armed. They are obeying their own laws, whatever they are, and look at us with distrust. As has often been said, we are the intruders here. To grasp this region is to grasp the tide of life itself. By the way, we have given up the Land Rover and are proceeding on foot, no fewer than ten miles a day. Also, by the way, I had a boyfriend from our group but he's gone now. I'm glad of that. He was so insistent. You were never insistent, at least insistent in the way he was insistent. I can see us now, you and me, more clearly now. Can we begin again? Will you come to me?

Ned read the cable in a state of high alarm, remembering El's voice, its timbre, its velocity. And all this time he felt her hand on his arm, her mouth close to his. She was whispering something. He glanced again at the cable, long lines of type. She spoke of the gorgeous sunsets, a blood-red sun against the darkening sky. Oh, you have no idea. He heard her voice, ever so slightly hoarse. And in the morning the reverse, she wrote, the country lights up so slowly you can feel it on your skin, the heat rising, and you believe you are in paradise . . .

Ned stepped to the window. The time was late fall, a windy Saturday, leaves flying in the street. The room was silent, Mahler having vanished, and he hadn't even noticed. Two girls passed under his window. They were arm in arm and laughing, a companionable moment. He was trying to imagine Elaine's "region," where it was precisely and what they were doing there besides walking and dodging wild beasts. He wondered if they sang while they walked, like the Volga boatmen. Ned held Elaine's cable in his hand while he watched the street. The voice was not hers. The sentences were headlong, racing one another to some imaginary finish line. He had rushed through the cable and now he looked at it again. She wrote that she was arms-qualified, quite at ease with her Winchester. She had bought Ray-Bans with amber lenses. For the time being they were not shooting anything, content to watch the animals dance. She ended her manifesto with an expression of love and an apology for the way they had parted, her harsh words. She hadn't known quite what to say. Well, it was not a matter of what to say but how to say it. She had let him down. She knew that. But she wished desperately for a reconciliation. The fates intended it. The final sentence was in a language Ned did not understand, probably Swahili. It ended, All my love, Your Baby. Baby? He had never called her Baby because she was not the sort of woman you called Baby. He called her Elaine or El, sometimes Elly. Once he called her Blue-Eyes and she laughed and laughed.

Ned took a step back, still looking into the street with its bright fall colors and the afternoon yet to reveal itself. He looked once again at the cable. There was no return address, unless the cable office in Nairobi was the return address. He wondered how you got there. No doubt the jumping-off place would be New York, then London to Nairobi. Ned's mind was unsettled, thinking about Nairobi and the person who wanted to reenter his life. And what had happened to Cape Town? His life was not a revolving door. The first part of the cable he had understood well enough and had been tantalized by it. The rest of it was not the Elaine he knew. There was only so much you could know of another, just as there was only so much you could know of a news event. The one thing known for certain was that the first version was wrong. The second and third versions were also wrong, but less so.

He thought Elaine had gone off the deep end. He heard her voice but could not see her whole. They had been apart for the best part of a year, and no word from her except one wretched postcard. One postcard and now this: a summons from the back of beyond. She wished him to join her at once, as if he were free to do so. As if he were untethered, his newspaper world a kind of hobby like stamp collecting. He had made a life for himself and for the moment could imagine no other. Certainly not one in east Africa.

He looked at his watch and thought he would go to the office, see about the Sunday paper. But he did not move, continuing to stare at the street, now without foot traffic. He wondered what it would be like, being charged by a rhinoceros. What did they weigh, anyhow? A ton. Probably not much more than a ton. Ned was not fleet afoot. Neither was he Winchester-qualified. When he was a boy he owned a pellet gun, good for squirrels. There were squirrels everywhere beyond the Herman cemetery. A squirrel paradise. What was the justification for killing a rhino? The horn was valuable. The Chinese thought it an aphrodisiac. So that would be one justification, enhancing the sexual pleasure of the Chinese multitudes. He wondered if El thought about this when she was lining up a shot. And was the horn equally provocative to women?

When the telephone rang he was startled and moved quickly to pick up at the second ring. It was his Sunday editor, reminding him of the president's news conference at eleven. Ned threw on a jacket and quitted his apartment for the office, a twenty-minute walk, thinking all the while about Elaine and her one-ton rhino. He did not know how to respond to her. No doubt she was lonely; black rhinos could take you only so far in life. He believed he had a responsibility toward her and he did not know what to do, how to respond. Judging from her cable, she had had a life-altering experience in Africa and this experience drew her toward him once again. She wished to resurrect lost time. The interim was a bridge into the past when they were together and compatible. Africa's raw edges had carried her back to Astor Street where they could pick up where they had left off. The plains of Africa were an epiphany, a reordering of her world. Not their world, her world. She had turned the page. Today was tomorrow, and the truth was, she had left him behind. He was in the present moment and she was a step ahead. Ned returned the cable to its envelope and the envelope to his desk drawer, the one with the lock. He stood at the desk a moment, tapping his finger on the glass surface, and then he left for the office.

Ned Ayres stood in his office facing the glass wall that looked into the newsroom. He always thought of his office as an aquarium, but in this instance the fish were outside. The ceiling lights were as bright as a supermarket's. His mood had improved the moment he walked into his office: the sofa, the coffee table, the refectory table with the most recent editions of the Chicago, New York, and Washington newspapers lying flat. A photograph of his parents had pride of place on the big desk next to the Royal typewriter and a coffee mug crammed with number-two pencils, including the one pencil with blue lead. A sketch of his friend Caroline Browne completed the ensemble. Caroline was a singer in great demand at Chicago's North Side cabarets. They had had a brief romance, convenient because they kept roughly the same hours. The romance flourished and then ended when Caroline moved to the West Coast, a film opportunity she could not pass up. The sketch was done by an English painter much in vogue. Caroline's pout reminded him of Piaf. She wanted him to come to L.A. for a long weekend but he had not yet found the time.

Then his door opened and the Sunday editor looked in to say they were ready to convene the morning meeting, unusually contentious because there were so many candidates for page one, even a sports yarn that was droll. A frog-jumping contest in Grant Park.

Begin without me, Ned said.

Are you all right, Ned? The Sunday editor looked at him strangely.

I'm fine. What do you mean?

You look as if you had seen a ghost.

No ghosts, Ned said. I'll join you in a minute.

We have this train wreck and a killing on the West Side. Washington has a story about an ambassador's confirmation, suddenly in deep trouble. Another girl problem. God, men and their zippers. Thing is, he's from here. LaSalle Street lawyer. Lives very grandly out in Lake Forest.

I said I'll be there. Go away.

Aye-aye, Cap, the Sunday editor said, and closed the door. Ned watched her go, moving her hands from side to side as if drying them of sweat, a mute announcement that Ayres was in a foul mood, unusual for him, so even-tempered most of the time. That was true enough. His life was orderly for the most part, seven-day weeks, twelve-hour days. He believed himself in charge of an alternate universe that demanded his full-time attention. His personal life, such as it was, did not interfere. In its own way editing was soul work, a deeply mysterious business. Page one, properly designed, was often a work of art, the lead story under a three-column headline and over a two-column explainer, news analysis, a photograph above the fold. The paper was fresh each day, a kind of miracle. The weather report was fresh. The obituaries were fresh. The box scores and the stock tables were fresh. The comics page was not fresh. Instead, it was familiar. That was its value, a page to go to and not be surprised. The comics page was consolation, along with the editorial page with its cartoon and roster of columnists, biased views nicely balanced. Ned watched the conference room door close and knew that he would have to move quickly. But he did not move, thinking once again of Elaine and her long cable. No doubt she was lonely.

Ned buttoned his coat, remembering that Caroline Browne was not enthusiastic about news. She thought of it as a product like soap flakes or toothpaste, something bought over the counter for a specific purpose. In her case, the film reviews. Nothing else.

Ned looked up, stirred at last, opening his door and moving swiftly to the conference room, where he sat in his usual seat at the head of the table, taking charge. The LaSalle Street lawyer went on One, below the fold. The West Side killing was inside. The train wreck, near Carbondale, led the paper. The frogs went on One, below the fold. Ned always spoke in a low voice, barely audible at the rear of the room. The Sunday editor disputed the train wreck: Hell, Ned, there are only two dead and a dozen injured. Readers are drawn to train accidents, Ned said, looked at his watch, and left the conference room, not before telling the Sunday editor that she could do what she wanted with the president's news conference, but in Ned's opinion it belonged inside. Somewhere in the vicinity of page eight.

Later that year, in the winter, Ned received a three-line telegram informing him that Elaine was dead after a brief illness, a virus of unknown origin. On the advice of the doctor her remains were cremated and buried in the cemetery on Nairobi's outskirts, not a suitable place but all there was. Ned closed his office door and stood staring at the flimsy yellow paper. It was sent from east Africa, some city he never heard of, from someone whose name was unpronounceable. He wondered if they had managed a Christian service. He heard a tap at the door but did not look up. His breathing was shallow and he felt lightheaded, his vision aswim. In their time together Elaine had never been sick, not even a common cold. Ned's thoughts were every which way. Time came to a full stop, and when it resumed he walked unsteadily to his desk and made the call to the obit man and told him to come to his office at once. And when the obit man inquired into details, Ned was surprised at how little he knew of her. He did not know her birth date. He did not know her mother's maiden name. He said to the obit man, You do the detective work.

Ned arranged the memorial service and delivered the eulogy, a slow-rhythm affair that lasted but ten minutes. He talked about her spirit, her courage, and her love of the outdoor life. Elaine was not from Chicago, but her friends were there, many of them attached to the university. Mostly they were strangers to him but a few made a point of approaching him to say how much they would miss Ellie, her skill at backgammon, her obsessive knitting, her mimicry. Ned smiled and nodded as if he were fully familiar with these hobbies. He was not familiar with them, except for the mimicry. Eleanor Roosevelt. Adlai Stevenson. But the atmosphere was desultory, and as soon as they decently could, Ned and Elaine's heartbroken father took a cab to the Loop and Ned's club, where they drank one whiskey after another. The club had all the vivacity of a mausoleum but the service was prompt. They were surrounded by portraits of the city's nineteenth-century founders. Elaine's father, Michael Ardmore, was a man of considerable personal charm, though somewhat the worse for wear physically. He was stooped. His complexion was sallow and his fingers trembled. He had a lion's long-jawed, flat-nosed head swarming with silver curls. Elaine had inherited the curls. Also, she had inherited her father's husky parade-ground voice, minus the continental inflections. They were alone in the club bar, hunched over the small cocktail table like two conspirators. Michael asked Ned if he had been in touch with Elaine, and Ned replied that he hadn't been. He had written but Elaine had not responded except for one cable that he found incoherent. He had not written back. He had not known what to say except that he missed her. And he was uncertain of the address. Maybe there was trouble with the post, Michael said, and Ned agreed, perhaps there was. Letters or cables lost in transit or confiscated by the authorities.

Ned raised his hand and in a moment the bartender was at his side, nodding and promising two more of the same. Michael watched the barman's retreat. Ned was lost in his own thoughts, considering the question of Elaine. He had decided a year ago that she was a one-way street, a cul-de-sac really. She inhabited another world, one difficult of access. He said this aloud and Michael shook his head and began to tell his own stories, enchanted tales of his daughter's childhood, her off-the-charts IQ and her determination to go her own way. Her pranks, her unreliable boyfriends — not you, Ned. Her reading habits, which did not include his own books. He loved her to death. She had written him about Ned, his lust for the news business, how fond she was of him. She thought the news business was a distraction. She said you were settled down.

Do you have a lust for the news business?

I suppose I do, Ned said.

It amused her, I think. I'm afraid she thought it a joke.

That's one way of putting it, Ned said with a conciliatory smile.

Ned cleared his throat and said, So you got letters from her.

Only the one letter, and not lately, Michael said. It worried the hell out of me. What was she doing? He paused and continued, She was so headstrong. I think she got that from her mother, an impossible woman but delectable. She was a handful. I was crazy about her until she became impossible. She was a beautiful woman but, as she said, serious beauty takes you only so far. She insisted it was tiresome listening to men tell you how beautiful you are. At first you don't like it and then you come to depend on it, a compliment from every quarter. That was the world according to Dutch. She said it was hard to make friends and harder still to keep them.

That would be the jealousy factor. Men were no better but they had the advantage of ugliness; a mournful or repulsive countenance attracted a certain kind of woman. Of course the ugliness had to go along with an unnatural confidence, meaning an air of mastery. Dutch was my second wife. My present wife, Tre, is a beaut. I couldn't live without her, or at least live successfully. She has final edit on all my books. Ned opened his mouth to inquire into the books and the advantages of ugliness but Michael Ardmore had a question. He ran his hands through his curls, all the while shaking his head. Tell me this. What in the name of God was Ellie doing in Africa?

Hunting animals, Ned said. Exploring.

Africa's a mystery to me, Michael said. She was on safari?

Rhino and elephant specifically. She liked the unspoiled terrain. I think she meant African naturalness.

Damnedest thing, Michael said.

In her way she was searching for a life. Something to believe in, maybe.

Michael snorted. Sometimes the truth is not present. It takes a hike. At other times it comes in disguise. Surely, Ned, you of all people would know that. Immersed, as you say, in the news. So you kill a rhino. So what.

The truth is always there somewhere. Otherwise—

Otherwise what?

You're confounded.

That's usually the way. Searching for something that isn't there. Things are often—imperfect. Obscure. What you're left with is a damp stack of wood. No fire, not even a spark. Michael laughed and held up his hand. Or an empty glass, he said, to which Ned smiled and signaled the barman.

Exploring, Michael said sadly. That's one of the things Elaine did as a child. Got into trouble for it, too. She liked to snoop. That was another thing that drove me crazy. I never did anything about it because she was never malicious. And she made me laugh. I can't imagine her gone. She never said goodbye. And I didn't either. Inconsiderate of her. Me, too. Michael shook his head and looked at the ceiling as if he expected to find her hovering like a ghost. The barman came with two drinks, then went away. Michael said, You're a career man, aren't you?

What do you mean?

You love your work. Love it to death. Can't live without it.

Yes, that's true.

Must've been hard with Elaine.

Yes, it was.

There was a sudden noise as three men tumbled through the front door, the one next to the bar. The room filled up with loud voices and rough laughter. They had been to the Bulls game, another loss but a great game all the same. They draped themselves over the bar, demanding whiskey. All three lit cigarettes. The barman greeted them by name as he busied himself with the whiskey. One of the men looked over, saw Ned, and gave a laconic salute. Ned saluted back and their voices dropped an octave. Ned explained that the saluter was a well-known political lawyer, a friend of the mayor's.

They'll be out of here in five minutes, Ned said. What they have to say is not for a newspaper editor's ears.

Private business, Michael said.

Private business meaning city business, Ned said. They sat in silence, Ned wondering why anyone would name a daughter Dutch. Then he said, What kind of books do you write?

Novels, Michael said.

You're lucky. You don't need to fact-check. You don't need

47

sources. You can simply—make it up. And hope that the reader buys in, no?

Not always simple, Michael said. But I see your point.

Ned was quiet a moment, then decided to take his thought a step further. He said, In my business we have these conventions that seem quaint to outsiders. Take the word "plunge." A woman stands on a roof and an instant later lies broken in the street below. No eyewitnesses, or none that we are aware of. The point's this: She didn't fall. She didn't topple. She didn't drop. Those words imply agency. They imply carelessness, a stumble, a fainting spell, perhaps suicidal intent. Or foul play. Perhaps an unseen hand, but we do not know that. So the word is plunged. Plunge is immaculate. One moment she's standing on a rooftop, the next dead in the street. And that's all the reader is entitled to. The reader does not have carte blanche. The newspaper is not a restaurant where substitutions can be requested. The menu is prix fixe. In certain respects the newspaper resembles a straitjacket. Now if by chance there is an eyewitness, and that eyewitness gives a statement to the authorities, the reporter would be entitled to write that the victim jumped, was pushed, had fainted, according to police. And by the way, a redheaded stranger was in the vicinity. The cause of the plunge must be sourced, you see. Ned's voice had risen and the lawyers at the bar were listening in.

Michael smiled. What if the cop is lying?

Sooner or later we'll find that out. And the context will change.

A burst of rough laughter from the bar, but neither Ned nor Michael paid attention.

Michael said, Governments lie as a matter of course. They call it statecraft, raison d'état, national security. When they get caught they have a ready explanation. Mistakes were made. So you'd have to be careful. I like the idea of an immaculate verb, though. An immaculate conception.

Ned lit a cigarette and sat back in his chair, listening to Michael Ardmore's amendment. He was very sure of himself in a casual way, a wink and a smile. Washington was evidently a common conversation among the expatriates in Capri. Ned had told no one of his new situation, but there was no reason not to tell Michael, father of Elaine. He said, I'll remember your thought. I've taken a newspaper job in Washington, deputy editor. The publisher and I get on very well. He's only a few years older than I am and wanted someone of his own generation in the newsroom. It bothered him a little bit that I've never worked in Washington but we agreed the city's a quick study. So am I. So the fit should be all right. Two quick studies.

Congratulations, Michael said.

It's time for me to quit Chicago. There's nothing to keep me here.

Michael raised his glass. To plunging, then.

Plunging, Ned agreed.

They sat for a moment without speaking. Ned wondered if he had made a mistake telling Michael of his plans. He surprised himself that he had. The announcement had not been made and no one knew of it. Ned was accustomed to keeping things quiet. Still, he was correct in saying there was nothing in Chicago to keep him there. He looked up when Michael cleared his throat.

He said, I'm not sure actually that Washington's a quick study. All those competing interests. All that scrutiny, not that scrutiny changes anything. It's a gray city, Ned. It's not Renoir, it's Goya. Goya inside and out. For a while the papers were happy to collaborate with Renoir but that time is past. It's pretty much Goya all down the line, thanks to Indochina. I think you will find Washington—Michael thought a moment—not spontaneous, he said. Of course I may be wrong. It's been years since I've been there. Maybe Washington's changed. Alas, maybe it's only more so. They do think well of themselves in our capital. Modesty seems to be one of the casualties.

The barroom had fallen quiet. The lawyers had paid up and left. Ned and Michael Ardmore nursed their drinks in silence. The bartender looked at them but Ned shook his head. Michael rose from the table, saying he had to use the men's. His step was unsteady. He paused once, his hand on one of the cocktail tables to collect himself. Ned watched him go and had the sudden thought that this would be their last meeting. Michael would disappear into Italy and that would be that. His step was more secure on his return. Michael sat down heavily and said, Where are you from, Ned?

Indiana, Ned said, and went on to describe Herman and life there but did not mention the comedian. He said the town was in decline. His parents were gone now and he doubted if he would ever return. Ned said, I don't think of myself as being from any specific place. My hometown is wherever the newspaper is. Indianapolis is one sort of town, Chicago another. Now Washington. And Herman, of course. It's all one to me.

The waiter arrived with a chit, announcing that the bar would soon close.

Nice club, Michael said. Good service. I'm glad we had a chance to talk at last, speak privately, sort things out. If you ever get to Capri, look me up.

I will, Ned said. Do you know, I've never been abroad. I've never been to the West Coast, either. Or the Southwest. Or Canada.

Michael smiled. I'm sure you'll find Washington to your liking, the whole world crushed into a very small space. Sometimes a dungeon into which no light shines. But you can make something of that, too.

Ned sneaked a look at his wristwatch. The time was eleven p.m. The vast room was in deep shadow, illuminated only by the brace of low-watt sconces on each wall and a crystal chandelier overhead. The bartender was reading the racing form, a pencil between his teeth. Ned remembered that Elaine liked the races, Arlington Park on a sunny Saturday afternoon. She rarely won but liked the atmosphere. Then Ned had the fantastic idea that Elaine was nearby, listening from the shadows. She was wearing a white, long-sleeved shift and was barefoot. She was frozen in a kind of ethereal glow and her lips were parted as if she were about to offer a thought of her own. From the street below Ned heard an ambulance siren, fading away. Then Elaine faded away, too.

You were in her heart, Michael said. I know that.

And she in mine, Ned said. Probably for good.

Don't say that! said Michael, his voice rising. Why, you're a young man. You've got decades ahead of you and you're going to an unfamiliar city, our capital, a wholly different world from the one you're used to. A different cast of characters. Trust me. I know these things. You've got a fresh start and you're young enough to take advantage. Someone else will come along.

Someone else did come along, Ned said.

Well, then—

She's in California now.

Terrible place, Michael said.

She's a singer. And an actress. She's a singer-actress.

They can be unreliable, Michael said.

So they can be, Ned said, finishing his drink and moving to rise.

But Elaine's father, staring into the middle distance, stayed put.

I hate it, he said. I hate it that she's gone. That she's buried in some place I never heard of and that I wasn't there to say a few words and perhaps better understand what joy she found in east Africa. Perhaps joy isn't the word. It's some other word, I don't know what. I was all she had left in the way of family, blood kin. Her mother died when she was a tyke. But of course you know that. She learned at a young age to look after herself. And when she was ten she was struck by polio, a year of struggle with that, and at last the polio went away, leaving no side effects. But it was a hard year for her. It left her wary. She believed the polio could return at any time. No matter that the doctors said no. I would say the polio left a shadow on her spirit. She became defensive. And also fatalistic. No wonder she liked Africa.

Polio, Ned said.

You didn't know?

No. Nor her mother's early death. She never spoke of it.

People are incomprehensible, often.

Evidently, Ned said.

Ellie and my second wife did not get on and that caused some tension, but we all learned to live with it. She went away to university as soon as she could and the university became her life. Many times she did not return home at vacation time but spent it in the library or with friends. She liked Thanksgiving, though. The ceremony of it. The toasts, the bottles of prosecco. She had a million questions about the Italian way of life, manners and, to the extent there were any, morals. I told her the Italian way of life did not project. Or if it did, it projected in farce. The Italian way of life was successful only in Italy. Nowhere else. Do you know what they're good at? Friendship. And they take the long view of things. Elaine never quite got it. She was an American girl through and through, and even though I was not an attentive father we got along fine when we were together. We liked the same jokes:

"Chancellor Adenauer visits Paris and is obliged to answer questions at customs:

Nationality? German. Age? Ninety-two. Occupation? Nein! Only for ze weekend."

Michael smiled but it took a moment for Ned to get the joke. Michael said, She was never much interested in my writing life. I don't know why. Maybe my books were not serious enough for her, or were serious in an unfamiliar way. I wish I knew where she was buried. But that will be an eternal mystery to me . . . Michael Ardmore's voice trailed off. He had lost his way. He exhaled, then raised his unsteady hands and let them fall. He said, I will never travel to Africa. I have no experience in Africa. Her grave and its location would be unfamiliar to me. It would be like visiting a stranger.

Michael said, I felt her presence a moment ago.

Yes, Ned said. So did I.

Perhaps a condolence.

Ned said, Elaine adored you. She thought you lived a colorful life and let nothing interfere with it. She called you My Papa.

I know, Michael said miserably.

Ned signed the chit. He had one last inquiry and said to Michael Ardmore, Can I ask where your material comes from? Methods and sources. You begin a novel. I imagine you have the first sentence, perhaps a paragraph in your mind, and beyond that a vast counterpane of blank pages. Where else does it come from besides your own head? From what you have said, I gather that facts do not govern. What governs?

Michael laughed, a derisory laugh without humor. He said, I govern. Something falls out of my mind and lands on a page. You read something in a book or a newspaper and it gives rise to something familiar, something in your life or another life. Someone tells a joke that reminds you of another joke or the same joke reworked. The reworking does not bring you closer to the actual event; it takes you farther away. That's the essence of it. Nothing is safe from your scrutiny. Perhaps the better word is sacred. Nothing sacred here, only a story that wants telling if you can reach the heart of it, this task that has to fit the grail you have set for yourself —revenge, say, or virtue. Or more likely, both at the same time. You collect stories that you will never use because they are exaggerated and belong to the common speech, a bar confidence that is enthralling but lies dumbstruck on the page. It is outlandish. Too funny to be true. In any case, it lies uneasily on the page. It is an ill-fitting suit of clothes. Sooner or later an emotion must arise, the death of a child or an old woman or a drunk in a bar. "What is our innocence, what is our guilt? All are naked, none is safe." Nothing is safe. Nothing is sacred. Not one thing. Much of the time the novelist is in a dream world. That would be hallucination with some drama. But I don't think that's an answer to your question. One answer is this: I don't know a single rule in the writing of fiction that stands scrutiny, save one. Believe in your material. Trust it as you would trust a barometer or a compass or the tide tables. The atomic clock. When something is wrong with a passage, rewrite the passage. Rewrite it fifty times if need be and in that process your story changes: he becomes she, and Capri becomes Chicago. Something like *Mourning Becomes Electra*. Rewrite the thing until it has a pulse, a beating heart. That's it. The one rule. The facts do not govern. I govern. The rest of it is eating and sleeping and dreaming and waking and working and sleeping.

Ned was silent a moment. He said, That does not happen in the newspapers. Something is printed. We call it a "piece." It's a double

54

meaning. It's factual enough and sometimes it causes great harm. That is not its intent. But it's the result. This comes as a surprise. No one expected harm. My God, you think, what have I done? In all innocence. But innocence is not the excuse. Innocence is the cause. And we are appalled, those of us who are in charge. The others turn the page.

Tell me more, Michael said.

Another time, Ned replied.

They parted on the sidewalk, promising to stay in touch. Michael said, When we meet again you must tell me about your "piece" that was "factual enough." Will you do that?

Ned did not answer. Instead he hailed a cab and helped Michael Ardmore inside. The old man appeared to be falling asleep, his eyes closing and his arms crossed on his chest. Until then, Ned said, and walked away up Michigan Avenue toward the Chicago River, head bowed against the north wind, a Canada or Minnesota wind rushing in from the lake. Ned knew there would be no "then." Then was none of Michael Ardmore's business, and he would not understand it in any case because it bore no relation to a compass, a barometer, the tide tables, or the atomic clock. Nothing mechanical, only wretchedly human. Then was out of bounds.

The street and the sidewalk were vacant at midnight. He began walking and soon enough came upon a derelict in the doorway of a bank. The derelict was huddled in a shabby sleeping bag that looked too small for him. His head rested on a worn overcoat, yesterday's newspaper stuffed into one of the overcoat pockets. Ned took a ten-dollar bill and slipped it between the derelict's fingers and fussed with the overcoat until the bill was concealed. A nice surprise for a faithful reader. Ned marched on. Michigan Avenue looked as though it went on forever, not a pedestrian in sight, the great stone buildings looming thick and impersonal. Like Stonehenge, they were difficult to distinguish one from another. And where were the druids? Now and again Ned saw a light in an upstairs window, a lawyer or an accountant working late. Perhaps a cleaning woman thinking about the midnight bus to the South Side, at that hour filled with bone-tired cleaning women, the air sweet with disinfectant.

Ned stepped carefully across Madison Street. Snow came with the north wind. He wished he had taken gloves with him. He paused to look across Michigan Avenue at empty Grant Park, a wilderness of shadows. The only moving things in the street and beyond were snowflakes. Ned buried his chin in his coat collar and soldiered on, thinking once more about the story that was factual enough. An ugly story, cruel at its heart, all but forgotten now except in the memories of its participants. Ahead of him a Yellow cab dipped its lights and turned the corner. Ned's feet were cold. Everything inside him was cold. His heart was frigid. He was approaching the Chicago River now, his office only steps away. He looked left and right, no cab in sight. The river waters were dark and tumbling slowly. He decided to detour to the office for its warmth and familiarity. There was always someone about in the newsroom, all lights switched on, the teletype from AP and UPI rattling away. Somewhere in the world there was breaking news, too late to appear in the morning paper. The late edition was long off press. He thought of himself as the last occupant of Chicago.

In moments he was in his office, shucking his overcoat and warming his hands at the register. They were crabbed hands, an old man's hands, big-knuckled. The newsroom was near empty, the two late men playing cards at one of the back desks, waiting for the telephone to ring, a fire or a killing. Ned poured a pony of Ballantine's, put his feet on his desk, and commenced to brood.

He thought of Elaine Ardmore and her father. Michael had lived too long in Italy. His opinions were cockeyed, but what else would you expect from a Capri world view? Expatriates were usually unreliable. They were especially unreliable when assessing the merits and demerits of America. Too much sun, too much prosecco. Too many lazy afternoons on a beach or on the fantail of a boat. America required reporting from the inside, shoe leather stuff. Nothing sophisticated about it. Pencil, paper, shoe leather. That was the beautiful thing about shoe leather reporting. It discouraged speculation. The facts took you only so far, and when the facts were exhausted you stopped typing and handed the piece to the desk. The desk arbitrated. Changed a verb, eliminated a redundant sentence, cut the last adverb, sent it downstairs.

Strangest thing, not knowing of Elaine's polio. Occasionally she complained about bad knees, but so casually he never thought about it except to ask if she wanted an aspirin. He remembered her lightly massaging her knees, a sour expression on her face. Somewhere along the line he had decided she was not marriage material. Neither was he. Still, he was unable to get her out of his memory. She was stuck there like a nervous tic, part of his private repertory company, like Uncle Ralph and his mother, who knew a beautiful man when she saw one.

Then Ned was home, on the doorstep fumbling for his keys, his hands clumsy in the cold. Ned Ayres was disoriented. He was tired and stooped like a cleaning woman in the Loop. He counted the twelve steps to his apartment, grateful for the sudden warmth. He turned on all the lights and looked carefully at the bookcase on the long wall. He supposed he had a thousand books, mostly histories and biographies, and was too tired to read any of them. But the books were a comfort. Ned had vacation time coming and planned to go south for a week and take half a dozen books with him. He thought about a nightcap and decided against it, then said the hell with it and poured a finger of scotch into the Lalique glass Elaine had given him on his birthday. He stood at the window, watching the snow gather below. The streetlamp cast a wan glow but not so wan that Ned was unable to see the couple necking, pressed against the hood of a blue Cadillac. He watched them a moment, thinking that it would make a wonderful photograph for the paper, page one for sure. Necking as the snow fell on Astor Street in Chicago, run the thing above the fold. There was a privacy question, but with their faces pressed together, they would be impossible to identify. And what would they think, picking up the paper on a Sunday morning and seeing themselves, caught unawares. Readers would love it. Romance in the snow.

Looking at them, thinking of Elaine, Ned remembered a quotation from somewhere:

The dogs bark. The caravan moves on.

Four

THE HABERDASHER

Ned ayres arrived in Washington a half hour before a spring snowstorm, a three-day affair that effectively closed the city. His flight from Chicago was the last plane in. He put up at the Willard Hotel, dined well, and rose the next morning to find a white city, no pedestrians, no cars, a few athletes on cross-country skis traversing Pennsylvania Avenue. Ned had thoughtfully brought snow boots and set out to look at the government buildings nearby, the Treasury and the White House, the Old Executive Office Building next to the White House, Lafayette Square across the street. No one was in the square. It was a ghost square, somnolent and pristine, newborn, Ned thought. He noticed that the White House driveway was cleared, then saw the guards who had cleared it, gathered around the sentry house next to the open gate drinking coffee. There was no wind. Ned was comfortable in his heavy coat and scarf, his fedora set at a Bogart angle. He brushed aside snow to sit on one of the square's benches and lit a cigarette. At ten in the morning most of the White House windows were dark. Then he observed two dogs cavorting on the lawn, LBJ's dogs, he supposed. They were the only moving parts in the vicinity. The White House had a southern plantation look to it. The snow around it was white and fluffy as cotton. The Old Executive Office Building resembled something in frigid St. Petersburg, two plainclothesmen in long coats and bearskin hats flanking the entrance. Ned thought of Cossacks. Still, a nineteenth-century atmosphere. Where were the men in top hats? A woman in crinoline? Ned felt a surge of well-being, as if the nation itself was asleep and without care. He looked around him and believed at last he had found his place in life, and in the nation's capital of all places, a city on a river, the American flag limp on its standard, snowed in.

Ned Ayres saw at once that the city remained preoccupied by the assassination. The dead president's ghost was the context. What would Kennedy have done? Did he have a secret plan? His many able assistants remained in government, in the various departments and the White House itself. They felt obliged to support the new man, keep him on track to advance the martyr's legacy. But they were diminished in spirit, objects of sympathy. They were yesterday's men. In some fundamental way they had lost confidence, in themselves and in their new president, whose anguish over the war dead was obvious to anyone who saw him up close. Things were unbalanced. No one spoke of the New Frontier. Events were in charge and the events lacked coherence. One thing did not lead to another in any logical sequence. That was owing to the ghost whose promise seemed so bright. Brilliant really. And that was all it was, a promise that was unfulfilled. The spoiled and remorseless gods of antiquity hovered over most every conversation. That was the true meaning of the fascination with conspiracy. Oswald was banal. His motives, to the extent that his motives were understood, were banal. His very life was banal. The capital seemed caught in the crux of a trash novel with many chapters still to come for the martyr, certain women and undisclosed health problems, but these were not, for the moment, fit to print. A familiar face was among them once again. Nixon.

Ned Ayres moved with circumspection, the better to earn the confidence of the newsroom. He was an unknown quantity, fresh from Chicago. Chicago politics bore little relation to politics in the capital, altogether more subtle, and of course more consequential. The foreign aid bill was not a tenement fire. Committee chairmen did resemble aldermen—why, some of them had been in power for decades. The House of Representatives with its arcane rules and procedures had nothing in common with the Chicago City Council except for occasional unruly debates. The press was not regarded lightly as it was in Chicago. The press was part of the scheme of governance. Important congressmen each had a reporter attached to him like a Seeing Eye dog, favors given, favors withheld, guidance. The same seemed to be true of the departments—the Pentagon, State, and Treasury. They all had their Boswells, all agreed on one simple principle: The work was important. It was the nation's business. Reporters carried with them an attitude of lofty seriousness unknown in Chicago. Was this seriousness a little too lofty for its own good? Perhaps. Dispatches from the State Department often employed the language of diplomacy, written by one man for one man—the secretary of state. The ordinary reader was often baffled. "Disingenuous dissembling." The crisp, clean lede was derided as simplistic. Ned watched all this for two months before he made his first move, adding one reporter to the Saigon bureau and removing one from London. The Saigon man was elated and the London woman was not. Her Belgravia friends would now be lost to her. But the staff approved: This Ayres knows what he's doing. And the ultimate tribute: He's one of us.

For Ned, the unfamiliar soon became commonplace. Within

a few months he was plunged into the city's lively evening hours, where the shadow government and its aspirants flourished. Ned found a suitable three-room apartment off Dupont Circle within walking distance of the newspaper and in due course was introduced to the writer Monica Rainer, who was drawn to a newspaper editor who came from Herman, Indiana, and had never been to college. Monica believed in the self-taught. She had grown up in Washington, the daughter of diplomats who had spent most of their careers outside the United States. Sometimes she accompanied her parents abroad, most times not. She had attended a boarding school in Connecticut and visited her parents in the summer, when it suited her. Really, she said, she had raised herself. Her parents had been wonderfully permissive. When Ned met her, she was a few years out of college and working as the weekend girl at one of the newsmagazines, earning enough to keep her own apartment in Adams-Morgan, where she wrote her articles and, as she said, watched the elephants dance. The year Ned met her, Monica had won a prize—not one of the big ones, but one of the good ones.

With Monica on his arm he discovered that Washington was loose, alert, and much more vivacious than he had expected. It had very little in common with Indianapolis and Chicago, let alone Herman. Monica observed that the workday usually extended well into the evening, work a kind of fetish, even for the press corps, or perhaps especially for the press corps. Why, one of her colleagues spent last Christmas Eve at the office, polishing a piece he had written the week before, destined for the New Year's issue. Mommy and the kids wrapped the gifts and trimmed the tree and sang the songs, and when he arrived home at last the drudge demanded—well, never mind what the drudge demanded, but it wasn't eggnog. Washington was worldly and hospitable in the manner of the old South. Negroes drove the taxis but were not much visible on the police force, let alone in the Foreign Service or the newsroom. During daylight hours the pace was serene or appeared serene. The clumsy blockhouse office buildings contributed to the serene idea, giving the impression that all was well, things under control. Monica laughed and dropped her voice an octave: You know what we say around here—what's past is prologue. Shakespeare's all-purpose remark. The press liked to think of itself as a necessary ingredient to all this, sometimes watchdog, sometimes lapdog, as much a part of the government as the Central Intelligence Agency. Requires a certain personality type, Monica said, curious, adaptable, ambitious, and subtle, not so different from the skills of a lawyer, minus the glam.

It would help if women were a part of this scene, but they aren't, except to keep the flags flying at home. And when you find a woman in the White House or on one of the national committees, as often as not they are as aggressive as the men. They have a word for it that somehow does not fit the bill. Resolute, yes. Brilliant, okay. Intrepid, brainy, all okay. Monica gave a theatrical sigh.

Not, however, tough. That's a man's word, tough. A bully's word also, I think. And the thing is, women buy into it. They think, It's a man's town, and if you want to compete you'd better speak the local tongue, and that includes toughness. And the next best compliment is, "She's got balls." Monica said, That's one of the things I don't care for about this town, the vernacular. The other is the locution "this town." They use that because they think of the capital as a village where only about two hundred people actually count. Drive the horses. Some truth to that, by the way. But not enough to excuse it. But that's me, Monica said, raising her eyebrows. And I'm well known for being behind the times. I like to rain on parades. You'd think writing articles in such an environment would be foolish. Don't believe it for a minute. We live in nature's realm, the survival of the fittest. Depends naturally on what you mean by fittest. How that's defined. And how the fates behave, meaning the alignment of the stars. And you, Neddy, you're in the middle of it now. Monica gave a kind of witch's cackle and turned off the bedside light, leaving the room in total darkness.

From the beginning, Ned Ayres saw the capital as a portfolio of secrets, hidden hands concealed by Oriental screens. Now and then the screens parted and hands were visible. A furtive handshake and the screens closed tight. That was how business was done and had always been done. Mark Twain and Charles Dudley Warner with their *Gilded Age* were on to it. Sometimes, listening to a confidence, Ned was reminded of Uncle Ralph and his war delusions. Ned tried to explain that to Monica, but it seemed his story did not travel, for she only smiled and said something to the effect that delusional behavior was run-of-the-mill in the capital. The rule as opposed to the exception.

Of course most everyone Ned met was from someplace else, to the point where it was customary to ask, Where are you from? And the answer was immediate: Ohio or California or Kansas. But such was the pull of the capital's magnetism that after a year or so the ancestral home receded as surely as dusk, and the response became, Well, Ohio, actually, but we're here now and intend to stay. Isn't Washington a beautiful city? It seemed that no one ever went home except former presidents. This was known informally as the Truman Rule. To most everyone else Washington was exciting and, more to the point, durable in a way that Cleveland was not. Washington was here today and most emphatically here tomorrow. No such thing as a labor shortage in the capital, and so the man who came aboard as legislative assistant to the senior senator stayed on after the old man's defeat or retirement, easing into a splendid law office where his knowledge of Senate procedures and the men who enforced them could be put to work at once. Their wives, the ones who were tough enough, often went to work for the government or a lobbying firm. Their eldest daughter managed a summer internship at one of the newspapers. All this did not begin yesterday, but it reached a summit during the Kennedy administration, stuffed with Harvard professors and other academics, school friends of the president. Old Democratic lions who believed their day was done were suddenly catapulted into an important embassy or the seventh floor of the State Department. These were the newcomers' neighbors, seen walking their dogs on N Street—and so the capital became a kind of fabulous village with wonderful markets catering to the many foreigners, diplomats mostly, the French and the Greeks and Brazilians and Cairenes and Japanese, and boutiques for women, not as glamorous as those in New York—that would come—but glamorous in their own way, particularly exciting when a shopper was notified that Jackie Kennedy was in the changing room.

All this transpired before Ned Ayres's arrival in the capital. But stories about that time were still told, and told fondly, as part of the golden age, gone now but very well remembered. Naturally Monica had another slice of that life. She stood at the window of Ned's apartment and pointed to Dupont Circle, the jewel of the capital's roundabouts, crowded with automobiles and a few pedestrians rotating on an enormous wheel. There were no roundabouts in New York, and if there were roundabouts in Chicago, Monica had never heard of them. Something European about the roundabouts, thanks to Monsieur L'Enfant. Of course the wheel had exits, but make a careless change of lane and you could be there, well, forever.

Monica said, Most people who had lived through that in Washington said that the Kennedy years were the happiest in their lifetimes. Cheap sentiment? No. They were sincere. The capital was alive in a way it had never been before or since. It was a privilege to work in the government and a privilege to write about it. A privilege to have been there. But now, for some, it was time to go home, retreat to Shaker Heights or Cambridge and look for a second act.

Monica had explained all this as a prelude to her announcement that she was going abroad to Cyprus where her parents were stationed. Ned was startled. His first thought was that Monica seemed to think that the world was something you got out of the way of, e.g., dreary Nicosia. Monica told him she believed she was losing herself in Washington, as if the capital were an insatiable organism that had to change form in order to thrive. Monica was bookish, too, so Ned was not surprised when she described the city as "one of the dark places on earth," Marlow's remark at the commencement of *Heart of Darkness*. A resident had to embrace darkness, yearn for it, be fascinated by its mystery, and by mystery she seemed to mean the capital's many secrets. Monica was spare, a little over five feet tall, twenty-four years old, lovely rather than beautiful, a magnetic smile when she chose to use it. She had energy to burn. Monica found Ned most appealing when he talked to her about Herman, which he did often at her urging, wry anecdotes that turned into dapper satires. To Ned, monotonous Herman was far distant. Yet at times it seemed close enough to touch.

When Monica went away to visit her parents in whatever billet they had been assigned, she felt estranged from them and disengaged from Washington. She was neither here nor there. She received news that her new book of essays, *Rock Creek Park*, had two gratifying advance reviews. The subject of the collection was

Washington, and she knew now that she was temporarily burned out so far as the capital was concerned. She needed to be provoked by wherever she was living. That was what inspired her prose. She had to be part of it and at the same time wary of it, hence her weekend work at the newsmagazine. But she had squeezed that for all it was worth and now needed something different. Her idea was to fly to Cyprus and return as soon as possible to the United States, Kansas City, where she was born and where her grandparents still lived. She asked Ned if he wanted to come with her to Cyprus, beautiful island, meet her parents and take a sail around the eastern Med. When Ned said he could not break away she did not press the matter, and that seemed to disappoint him. She thought Ned did not have an adventurous spirit, if adventure was defined as getting out of the rut. Ned liked his rut as a stamp collector liked his albums. No need to move from the den. So she would fly to the island solo and return to Kansas City solo and meet up at once with her grandmother. Some material there, she thought. In Kansas City there would be no discussion of the Kennedy glam, years back now. She remembered a park on the fringes of downtown; that was where she would take an apartment, see how things thrived in Kansas City. Her grandmother was in her eighties but still in the pink, as she liked to say, full of stories about the old days, meaning the Depression and the war. Kansas City had long since won Monica's heart, an affectionate loyalty. Kansas City was modest, a good place to dwell for a while, find fresh material—well, she had the material, but it had to be excavated like ore. The Kansas River was picturesque, or that was how Monica remembered it. She was not a small-town girl. She was a small-city girl, an entirely different circumstance. She remembered her monthly luncheons with her father when she was a little girl, always at one of the downtown hotels, her father confiding in her, disclosing his plans to join the Foreign Service. We've got to bring Mom along on this, he said, because she's not convinced. Her father talked about living in the wide world for a change and wanted to enlist Monica in the effort. My agent provocateur, he said, and laughed. It turned out her mother had no reluctance, as she explained during one of the shopping expeditions in downtown Kansas City.

Monica told Ned she wanted to settle down for a while, and that meant leaving Washington. The way she said it put Ned in mind of a bad debt. Better to settle now than settle later, because interest was compounding. He was distressed, being forced to revisit his familiar problem. In order to pursue the romance he would have to reevaluate his own life and work, and this he was disinclined to do, at least just then. He was not truly interested in the things of his own life, preferring the lives of others. Monica's life, her "material," was infinitely more interesting than his own. He had no material. He edited material. At bottom Ned Ayres did not wish to compromise, and was not compromise the essence of married life? Or of any life shared with another. Married life had many virtues but compromise was always in first position, after the children had been put to bed. Now and again during his infrequent evenings alone he wondered if he would remain a bachelor, if that suited him in a way that a beard suited some men's faces and not others'. Hemingway. Lenin.

When Ned saw her off at Union Station—it was typical of her to travel by train, American scenery unspooling before her eyes —he was unable to find words. When she kissed him goodbye she had never looked lovelier. She was elated. Her mind was made up. She was traveling to the Med. Then she was going home.

She said, Ciao, Neddy. Stay well.

He said, You're unforgettable.

She said, No, I'm not, and gave a soft laugh.

Monica looked at him fondly. His shoulders sagged, his hands in his jacket pockets. Monica had used his slouch in *Rock Creek Park*, a pedestrian among the trees and the graves beyond the trees. Come to think of it, she had used his features in several of her essays, his crooked smile and Roman nose, his broad shoulders. That was the piece about men and cemeteries. She had invented a mustache and wire-rimmed glasses. The piece followed him on his rounds in Rock Creek Park, pausing at one gravestone and then another. She had him summing up, staring into the future. When he read it he did not recognize himself, although he liked the cadence. She had dedicated the book to him, Mister N. A. He was pleased at that. They had had such good times together. She never believed that they were permanent. His mind was always on his work, and she had to admit the same was often true with her, too. The difference was the difference between always and often. He allowed himself to be disturbed at any time if there was a crisis in his newsroom, one a.m. or five a.m. There were three people in their affair, themselves and the one on the telephone, Mr. Deskman. Standing at the window holding the phone, Ned reminded her of Buffalo Bill in e. e. cummings's great poem, riding a water-smooth-silver stallion . . . She thought he was fundamentally out of reach. So she knew that things could not continue as they were and Ned would never change. She had always felt safe with him. He had never mistreated her. She was not sure she was doing the right thing, traveling to Cyprus and then to Kansas City. She cared for her work as much as he cared for his, and perhaps that was the difficulty. Someone would have to yield, and it would not be her and it would not be him. Ned Ayres did not show the usual signs of fierce ambition, but they were all there, buried. In her darker moments Monica disdained the news, a kind of outside agitator. The mission that ruled his life and, by extension, hers. So here she was at Union Station ready to board the New York train. Nicosia, then Kansas City. She put her hands on his shoulders.

He said, Will you at least write?

I'm a bad correspondent, she said. But I'll send you a postcard of the harbor at Kyrenia. Little tiny harbor, one of the gems of Europe. If you think of Cyprus as Europe. Some do. We'll see. Then she turned her face from him, realizing how cold she sounded. He did not deserve that. She said, Of course I'll write. Let you know where I am. How things are going.

I wish to God you'd stay here.

He was not certain she heard his voice, so soft. The train was already in motion and she swung up the stairs like an acrobat and then she was gone. He noticed that she had had her hair cut, short on the sides and in back. He knew a makeover when he saw one. Ned turned and walked away into the heat of a Washington summer.

Ned missed her. He received one postcard: the Kyrenia harbor, as promised. He sent two letters in return but did not hear from her again. Mutual friends said she was back in Kansas City, loving it, at work once more. Then she, too, receded in his memory, as Elaine had done. His fortieth birthday came and went. The newspaper won two Pulitzer Prizes that year, causing the publisher to give him a block of stock as a reward. Ned discovered he was mildly rich, rich enough to afford a European trip in the grand style or something expensive at one of the Caribbean resorts. Neither appealed to him so he took a week on Mackinac Island, a quiet place that bored him, in part because he was alone. He had found a new girl, Angela Borne, but she was unable to get time off. Mackinac had what was said to be a nineteenth-century ambiance, horse-drawn buggies and the like. Most everyone there had small children in tow.

Every day he telephoned the paper for the latest news and gossip. He might as well have been in Cyprus without Monica. He spent much of his time reading Balzac's *Lost Illusions*, a savage satire of the mid-nineteenth-century Paris press. Hilarious, shrewd, perhaps overdone. Ned put *Lost Illusions* aside and bought a thriller, one of John le Carré's books, and found it engrossing. Le Carré was wonderful with atmosphere. Ned had the idea that a skilled novelist could bring something special to the newspaper, used strictly as an atmosphere man, someone to describe the feel of things and leave the quotes to a reporter. Well, not such a good idea. The reader wouldn't know where he was, the real world or a made-up world. Ned was sitting in a rocking chair drinking tea on the porch of his hotel. The newspaper was a bad place for a confusion of realms. Readers had enough trouble distinguishing between the news pages and the editorial pages. A novelist would glue it up for good. The idea was appealing, though, something fresh. Fresh as paint, as his mother liked to say. When the waiter arrived to see if he wished more tea, Ned said no and returned to Washington the next day.

He celebrated his return by taking Angela Borne to the symphony—wonderful orchestra seats, the secretary of the Treasury on Angela's left, the Berlin Philharmonic playing Mahler's Sixth, von Karajan conducting, a fine dinner later at the Occidental. And so to bed.

One autumn day in the election year 1976, Ned was in his office reading obituaries in the evening paper when he saw a two-column headline at the bottom of the page along with a studio portrait.

MICHAEL ARDMORE, 77
WRITER, SPORTSMAN

The obituary revealed nothing that Ned did not know except the "sportsman" part. It turned out that Michael was a celebrated fly-fisherman, celebrated enough that *Sports Illustrated* ran a profile of him, the profile most flattering. Ned remembered Michael's enormous hands and wondered whether fly-fishing had anything to do with that. Doubtless not. He remembered sitting in at an interview of a boxer in Indianapolis and how surprised he was at the boxer's hands, so small, almost dainty. Ned looked again at the obit. The cause of death was not given. He remembered that he had promised to tell Michael the story he had described as "factual enough." Another time, Ned had said, and they had parted on empty Michigan Avenue, the hour near midnight. They were both filled up with whiskey. Ned wished he had known about the fly-fishing. Ned himself had been a decent fly-fisherman in his youth, not that the Daggett River ever yielded much and what it did yield was inedible. But Ned had not fished in years, and he recalled now how much he liked the aesthetics of it, the circular flight of the fly, the unwinding of the line, the violence of the strike. There was no violence on the Daggett. The strike was more like a pinch.

Michael Ardmore was a thoughtful man, sure of himself. He had said, Trust your material. The atomic clock. Good advice when you were making things up, exploring possibilities, a typewriter the mother of invention. Michael Ardmore's findings didn't work in news, the material in doubt until verification. Never trust it from the beginning. Always remember: the first version is wrong. Not always. Almost always. Michael did not understand this concept. He did not value it. Well, he would understand it all right. But verification was irrelevant to him. He was his own verification.

"Factual enough" was the concept that interested Michael Ardmore.

. . .

Such a disturbing story, an off-the-rails story that asked forgiveness all the way around. That would be the long view, the sympathetic view, and far from universal. The story was published when young Ned Ayres was city editor of the Herman paper. Acting on a telephone tip, the reporter Gus Harding had learned that a well-known and well-liked businessman named William Grant had done jail time when he was nineteen, armed robbery of a gas station in Moline, Illinois, a Mississippi River town. The station attendant was badly beaten, "savagely" according to the police report. William Grant was swiftly caught and swiftly tried and sentenced to six years at Joliet, and when he was paroled he disappeared.

Gus Harding learned that Grant's name was in fact William Kelly. He had gone to court to legally change it, and it was as William Grant that he enrolled in one of the small Ohio colleges where he was given a full scholarship, having impressed the dean of admissions with his passionate interest in the writer Jack London. Like London, William Grant declared himself a socialist. He also claimed that at one time or another he had been a hobo, a hack driver in Boston, a lumberjack in Maine, a cowboy in Montana. All bogus, but enthralling to the dean. There was no biography like it at the small Ohio college, a student body composed mostly of farmers' sons and lawyers' daughters. If there was a socialist in the student body, the dean had never heard of him. Or her. Hobos, lumberjacks, and cowboys were also scarce. William Grant did not proselytize. His socialist sympathies were a private vice, an admirably adult way to go about things, as the dean observed when he recommended Mr. Grant for the scholarship. A remarkable young man, the dean said, another slice of the pie altogether. William Grant did very well at the Ohio college, dean's list from the beginning, a mysterious figure on campus. He kept mostly to himself. Of course he was years older than most of the students. He had certainly been around. When he was asked to give one of the commencement speeches, he declined. He did not speak well and was self-conscious about his appearance. William Grant was then thirty-two years old, conspicuously tall with a rolling gait and a badly scarred face that he attributed to a forest fire in Montana where he had volunteered to join the mountain fire brigade. Perhaps the dean had heard of the tragedy, five dead in the blaze. He himself was fortunate to escape with mere burns. His biography, what of it he chose to disclose, was appealing to the lawyers' daughters. Something dangerous about him. Something unpredictable. He was soft-spoken and discreet but could not disguise a certain dash. A man with a history, in other words. In later years he became a legend at the Ohio college.

It was as William Grant that he showed up one day in Herman and quickly made himself known. His rough appearance put some people off but his manner was quiet. He rarely raised his voice. Within the year he bought the men's store on Benjamin Franklin Boulevard, retitling it William Grant Haberdashery. He stocked the shelves with up-to-date goods, clothing and accessories—though not too up-to-date because this was, after all, Herman. But his blue button-down shirts were a novelty, along with a nest of bow ties. Grant himself dressed down, an ordinary blazer and gray flannel slacks, the better to show off the Hart, Schaffner & Marx double-breasted suits in gray and dark blue. Judge Ayres was one of Grant's first customers, and a number of the town's lawyers took note, and before long the haberdashery was a success. Grant's signature innovation was to offer a free bright red bow tie to any customer who bought a suit. He called the ties Jack Londons. His private joke.

William Grant carried himself with authority. He impressed everyone as an experienced man who could take care of himself.

Most everyone believed the forest fire story and no one guessed the truth: a knife fight at Joliet. Grant was good on the golf course and very good at the gin games later in the locker room. He rarely spoke of his past, his family, or his birthplace, and everyone assumed—well, he had taken some hard knocks. His manner discouraged inquiries. William Grant did very well in Herman and before long married one of the Elias girls. Their father was president of the First National Bank of Herman, certainly the richest man in town. Howard Elias's firstborn daughter was a pretty girl named Leatrice. The entire town, or that part of it living on the east end of Benjamin Franklin Boulevard, watched the courtship, William Grant arriving at the Elias front door dressed in one of his Hart, Schaffner & Marx suits with the signature red bow tie and carrying a spray of yellow roses, bound for dance night at the Daggett Golf Club. Leatrice was devoted to her husband. In time they had two sons and any Sunday morning could be seen en route to the Congregational church, where the boys—Eugene and David—sang in the choir. Home again, William Grant changed into hunting clothes, fetched his Browning over-and-under, and was quickly out the door. His boys begged to join him but their father said no, this was his private time. When they were older they could join him. But not now. Private time meant what it said. His Sunday afternoons were sacrosanct, like church. A different sort of church, a stroll in the natural world, and if he was lucky they would have a brace of pheasant for supper that evening. Leatrice watched this Sunday-afternoon ritual with a benign smile. Her father was a hunter, so she understood. He knew all about hunting. Come along, boys, let your father have his afternoon. Why, we'll go to the movies downtown. At that, William Grant sighed. He loved the movies.

• • •

William Grant's destination was always the same. He drove south one hour to a sparsely settled region in southern Indiana. The ground cover was good for pheasant but otherwise nondescript, low hills and farmland, not far from coal country. In any case, pheasant were not the point of the journey. The point was privacy. William Grant preferred the late fall and early winter but hunted in all seasons. His particular destination was a shallow defile that ran five miles or more, which he entered by an ancient path. There was never anyone in sight and Grant thought of the defile as his own, a private hunting preserve. Now and again he saw deer but never shot one. He had no interest in deer. He liked the defile for its solitude, its atmosphere somehow prehistoric. There were no signs of habitation, not a cigarette pack or spent cartridge in sight. He supposed the ancient path was a legacy of the Potawatomi Indian tribe, the tribe all but vanished now but abundant in the nineteenth century. The defile had its own personality, but the personality was well concealed, revealing itself in bits and pieces, a miniature swamp here, a fine stand of birches there. It wore a different face for each season. Leatrice always prepared a light lunch, sandwiches, an apple, a carafe of coffee. An hour in, he paused for lunch, eating slowly, sipping coffee, thinking about his life — more successful than he had ever imagined. A tour de force. He had recast himself. He had built himself from the ground up, had become well groomed, with a softer voice. He'd been mysterious as to his past, whereas his life now was an open book.

That was the trouble with it. He attracted snoops. His hair was short now, whereas before it had been longish. The one thing he could not change was his cowboy's lope, long strides, legs wide apart. He had put one over on them all right, his family, his neighbors. In the beginning he felt like an acrobat on the high wire, the unseen audience below holding its breath in anticipation of the stumble that never came. That was why they were there, looking aloft at the high wire, waiting for the fall. This had its own perverse satisfaction. He called it sublime, hope denied. Instead, there was disappointment. People had never wished him well, not even when he was a small child. So at the conclusion of his imaginary high-wire stroll William Grant stepped onto the metal perch and gave his audience a mirthless grin, more snarl than grin. He thought of the grin as a ricochet that hit the mark dead center. Somewhere in the audience were his wife and children, blank-faced. They too were awaiting failure. His parents were there also, and the idiot dean of the college who thought of him as white trash, a malleable bit of clay that could be re-formed. And he had a point: you could alter the façade but the inside of things remained the same. His father had thrown him out of the house when he was eighteen. Get a job, his father said. You're on your own. Don't come back. So William drifted into a life of petty crime until the gas station job went sour. Six years at Joliet, minding his manners, making it clear to his cellmates that he was not one of the joyboys, and when that didn't convince them he carved up the ringleader and let him know what would happen if he ratted to the authorities. Well, William Grant was safe now. He had made a secure life for himself and his family, food on the table, a fine house in the good part of town. A Chrysler for him, a Ford for Leatrice, his boys always well turned out, everyone in good health. William Grant took two bites of the apple and threw the core into the bush.

But always there was a price to be paid. He knew that from the beginning. Don't play their game. But now he had, and the result was his fine life. No question, he had surrendered. He had given up a vital part of himself and had taken a makeover. Businessman. Family man. Reformed. What would his father have to say about that? To hell with his father. The truth was, that was not how William Grant thought of himself, waiting on people, a salesman, a man who tended to business, quietly polite while he sold his suits and Jack Londons, and all this time he was aflame with rage. All of it was inside, a kind of moral furnace. His surrender was unconditional. His wife and children did not know him at all. They lived in a dreamworld. What was it called? The nuclear family. Well, it was nuclear all right. One day they'd find that out.

William Grant lit a cigarette and blew a smoke ring, a perfect O until it frayed at the edges and collapsed. He was sitting with his back to a tree, the ancient path ahead of him. It was pleasant in the open air, the beginnings of an autumn chill. He had money; he could disappear anytime he wanted. He tried to summon the faces of his wife and boys, rising in the morning and finding him absent, no note. Leatrice would think he had left early for work, but after a moment's thought realized that was nonsense. The time was six a.m., no hint of dawn. The Chrysler was gone. She waited an hour and did what she always did when things went awry. She called her father, groggy with sleep, soothing all the same. Not to worry. Maybe he felt like a ride in his car. Maybe a breakfast meeting with someone. William Grant was smiling now, spinning it out, the suspense of it. Soon enough Leatrice's father took charge, driving the boys to school and returning at once to sort things out, his tight smile that had worry behind it. Has he seemed unhappy? Any health problems? But in the back of his mind the old man was exploring the idea of a woman somewhere. Women of all ages found William Grant attractive, always so well disposed. That cowboy lope and scarred face, muscular arms, knotty smile, trustworthy. There was always the sense that William Grant had had another sort of life before he arrived in Herman and no one knew what that life was. So there was a measure of revenge there. Somewhere along the line William Grant had been wronged, and he was not the sort of man to forgive and forget. Leatrice's father did not know where to turn. Howard Elias had been a banker his entire adult life and knew from experience that men had secrets often of a surprising nature, though as he grew older very little surprised him, certainly not in Herman. Lives were tightly held in Herman, a town of closed doors. But the banker intended to make inquiries.

William Grant laughed out loud at the conclusion of his reverie. He had placed most everyone he knew on a proscenium stage, William Grant himself in the wings, the observer of his own life as others saw him. And a question had arisen. Was it time to reinvent himself once again, simply to prove it could be done? He could not say that he was bored. He sighed and said to himself, Play the hand you've dealt. He was aces over tens at least, probably better than that. No one knew anything about him. He was a lie from the socks up. Laughing again: they had no idea of the strain it was, particularly in the early days. He had worked up a slight southern accent and once or twice made a blunder of pronunciation; but it was only once or twice and no one noticed. Temptation was always nearby. The idea of a mistress was appealing. There were two opportunities, both requiring stealth. Herman was closed as a clam, everyone watchful. He should have an out-of-town mistress, then, perhaps one of the girls in Mill City, down the road. Mill City was a mischief city, most everyone out for a good time, one tavern after another and music to go with the laughter. Law enforcement left you alone. He laughed again, realizing that he could create a second façade, a Mill City façade, a black-hat façade to go with white-hat Herman. Well, no question about it. He had retooled himself once and could do it again, though there were undeniable risks. That was one of the attractions. Risk was his middle name. That was how he got on in life, assuming identities not his own, the world his stage. In Herman his life was regulated and any deviation from it would be noticed and commented upon, beginning with Leatrice. It had taken him months to reconcile her to his Sunday-afternoon rendezvous downstate, the defile in the forest. He once called it solitary Sunday afternoon and her feelings were hurt. He had joked her out of her hurt feelings, explaining that he liked to put food on the table. He was a hunter-gatherer. Hence the pheasant and occasional quail. That was what men did, hunt for dinner. It took him longer than he liked, explaining things to her. She was a banker's daughter and used to having her own way. At the end of the argument his voice grew cold, and she admitted, much later, that he had frightened her. He said he was sorry but there were times when she had to back off. He meant no harm to her or the boys. He merely needed a furlough. So the crisis came and went. But how would he explain evenings out? Evenings out were rare, rare enough so that he had forgotten the last time he had one. But there were ways and means.

No, the time was not ripe. He decided that for the moment he would stand pat, secure with façade one. That was how he would think of it. Façade two would be in reserve for Mill City. He would only have to keep the lid on a little longer. In the meantime he would have some fun assembling his fresh façade, commercial traveler, riverboat captain, retired actor, definitely a man of means. Perhaps an anodyne career: retired seaman. William Grant liked Jack London's résumé. Until then he would plod ahead with his store, making a damned good living, too. So he would wait a little longer.

William Grant surveyed the woods, listening. He heard nothing. The sun was hidden behind the trees and ebbing. This was his place. Chances were that no one else knew it existed. It was important always to have a place of your own, inviolate. A hideout, a kind of open-air one-man clubhouse. As long as he had the defile he would be all right. Sundays were quiet in the country, now and then the voice of a bird. The defile was the place to go when the world closed in. Old man Elias was one of the closers, always asking about the haberdashery, how it was doing, its profits. Of course he knew these figures. He was William Grant's banker, the company receipts in his vault. The old man was a meddler. He said once, You ought to branch out to Mill City. Not a chance, he replied. They don't wear suits in Mill City. It's an overalls town. And the old man backed off at once, not before a laugh and his comment, William, you're a snob! I never would've guessed it, and then backed off again when he saw the look on William Grant's face. That was the last time the banker mentioned Mill City.

William Grant carefully stubbed out his cigarette and field-stripped the butt paper. Leave nothing behind. He was in a good way now, having thought things through without interference. Now he had the idea, fleeting, that he would stop in to one of the Mill City taverns on the way back to Herman, surely lively on a Sunday afternoon. See what action there was.

At the sound of a rustle behind him William Grant froze, then slowly turned his head, knowing that he had an intruder. This had never happened before. He rose, moving quickly, and saw a red squirrel eating a nut. William Grant remained still. He slowly raised the Browning over-and-under and blew the creature's head off.

The tip came in a straightforward manner, a telephone call to *Press-Gazette* reporter Gus Harding. The caller refused to identify himself by name but promised a blockbuster story. A story with legs enough to reach Chicago and beyond. He proposed a meeting, not in Herman but in Mill City, a bar called the Good Times, you can't miss it, a neon sign. I'll be in the rear booth, the caller said. I'm the one in the baseball hat, the White Sox. His voice was insinuating. The man was in his forties, balding, thickset, a bushy goatee. Gus Harding slid into the rear booth, ordered a beer, and waited. The stranger identified himself as Fred, a longtime acquaintance of the man who called himself William Grant. Actually his name was William Kelly. Fred said, Now think a moment and tell me what comes to mind when you think of Grant and Kelly. Gus looked at him blankly and shrugged. Fred said, The movie stars, dummy. Cary and Grace. Fred went on to say that Billy Kelly was a fan of the movies, always wanted to be in one. Fat chance with that face unless it was one of those Frankenstein movies, and let me tell you, if they'd've asked him he would've jumped at it. Kissed their ass. Quite a piece of work is our Billy. Fucking fraud.

Gus sat quietly listening, his dislike of this Fred growing by the minute. Gus knew right away that Fred was one of life's losers, a grievance-sneer on his mouth. Gus said, So what's the story?

How much is it worth to you?

I don't know what it is. And whatever it is, we don't pay for it.

The hell you say, Fred said.

Gus Harding had taken his notebook and pencil out of his pocket and laid them on the table. Now he returned them to his pocket. He looked at his wristwatch. Time to leave.

Fred sat tapping a manila envelope on the table and then slid it across to the reporter. Go ahead, look at it. There'll be no charge. Gus looked at the envelope a moment before opening the flap and spreading the contents on the table. There were press clippings from the Moline paper, the crime, the arrest, the trial, the sentence. The photograph of Billy Kelly was indisputably of William Grant, a younger Grant, an unconvincing half smile on his scarred face. There were official documents also, a transcript of the brief trial at which Billy Kelly did not speak, claiming his right not to do so under the Fifth Amendment to the Constitution. The jury's decision, the judge's order, the parole board's finding. Gus skimmed the material, then read it carefully, Fred looking sourly at him all this time. With a sigh, Gus returned his notebook to the table and made an entry. He looked at Fred but did not speak.

There's your evidence, Fred said.

Why? asked Gus Harding.

Why what? Fred said.

Why are you doing this?

My business, Fred said.

It's my business now, Gus answered.

He owes me money, Fred said.

Why does he owe you money?

That is my business, Fred said. That's no concern of yours. He paused a long moment, looking hard at the reporter. At one time we were friends, he said. Billy Kelly and me. That's a shit thing to do to a friend, don't you agree? He's just a punk. That's all he'll ever be.

Gus nodded, a neutral nod, and turned to look at the documents once again, verifying names and dates. He had been a reporter at the *Press-Gazette* for thirty years. The work suited him, the marshaling of facts, their deployment on the page. He could deconstruct a police report in two minutes, write his piece in five. Truly, for the most part the job was a kind of paint-by-the-numbers. After a time it all became second nature. Controversy was rare in Herman. The publisher insisted that any doubt should be resolved in favor of the Republican Party, but that was politics, the normal thing for a small paper in a rural community in the Midwest. The idea was not to stir the pot but to keep the lid on. The word the publisher used was mature. Present a mature face to the world, a confident face that promised—well, lenience. Patience was a virtue. The paper saw itself as reliable, disinclined to go off the deep end. The publisher was insistent on that point. Point being, the paper was adult in its approach to the news. Now and then it was sentimental, finding space for the lost dog or the cat in the tree or the retarded boy who made Eagle Scout. Adult did not mean cynical or callous. Quite the reverse.

Gus Harding understood these principles in his bones. Once upon a time, Gus could have moved up to Indianapolis or Muncie, bigger stages, higher wages, but he had no desire to leave Herman, where his family had more or less flourished for three generations. He looked across the table at this Fred, who was scratching his goatee. This story would be different. This one had trouble written all over it even if all the facts were scrupulously accounted for. Gus listened to Fred drum his fingers on the table now that the goatee was tidy. Gus said at last, How did you find him?

That's my business too, Fred said. I'll tell you this much—it wasn't difficult. So you've got your story. Now run with it.

You knew Mr. Grant well, then. Tell me about him.

He's a shit, Fred said. He'd screw his own grandmother. And he's done very well with his little men's store, hasn't he? Married the banker's daughter, civic leader. Family man. Everyone's friend. No one bothered to look under the covers. That's quite a little town you have there, Gus. Herrrrrrman. You should rename it Gullible. Fred laughed. He's pulled the wool over your eyes and you never even noticed.

Gus Harding frowned. Seems to me Mr. Grant has played by the rules. He made a mistake and did what you're supposed to do. Paid his debt to society, went straight, went to college, graduated, made a new life for himself in Herman. He's a fine citizen, father of two boys.

Fred laughed. Well, your fine citizen knifed a man in Joliet.

Left him for dead. He was never caught. And what about his debt to me? Where do I come in? He owes me money. That's the debt I care about.

So speak to him, Gus said.

I wouldn't go near Billy Kelly. He's a tough hombre. He's vindictive. Look at that face of his. Tells you all you need to know.

Gus grunted but did not reply.

Billy had dreams, Fred said. Fancy dreams. But he's a common criminal. Too big for his britches.

Gus said, What dreams?

You read through the trial transcript. You'll find his mouthpiece calling him a fantasist. That was his word. Fantasist. Billy Kelly didn't live in the real world, boo-hoo. According to the mouthpiece. But the jury didn't buy it. The judge didn't buy it. No one bought it. So Mr. Billy Kelly did hard time. He's dangerous. And he's a shit. He's leading a liar's life. He belongs behind bars.

Gus shrugged uncomfortably. Being a shit's not against the law.

And you call yourself a reporter! A reporter who refuses to report!

That's what I do. I'm a reporter.

So you're not going to report anything about this. The material I've given you.

I didn't say that, Gus said. It's an interesting story. Human interest, you might say. Whether or not it prints, that's another question. Publisher's decision, way above my pay grade. I do have one last question. Where did the haberdashery come from? The story you've given me does not mention that. Men's fashions?

Billy always had his nose in a magazine, Fred said. Always looking at the clothes. He's a fairy, you know. Queer as a three-dollar bill.

. . .

85

The rendezvous between reporter and source ended shortly after that exchange. Gus left Fred in the Good Times, a sneer on his face, stroking his goatee, nursing his beer. Gus drove slowly the twenty miles to Herman, thinking about the story he had been handed. When he got to the newspaper office he sat for thirty minutes in his car, still thinking. He would verify the news articles and the court documents but he knew they were genuine. Fred was genuine, too, a genuine first-class bastard holding a grudge. The story about the money could be true or not true. Gus doubted it. He did not know William Grant well. They moved in different circles, to say the least of it. He had never been inside the haberdashery; the goods on offer were well beyond his budget. Also, he had no need of a three-piece suit. He remembered then that his wife had bought him a Christmas tie and that Mr. Grant had been most helpful. He wrapped the gift as expertly as any woman. That surprised her. He did not look like a man who could wrap presents complete with a little red bow. Gus himself had never heard a bad word about William Grant. Civic leader, family man, nicely summed him up. He was not a fairy. He didn't look like a fairy. Gus decided to keep that news to himself. Dirty linen.

So he would do his job. He would go to the office, sit at his desk, and write a story. And he would take that story to the city editor, young Ned Ayres, and Ned would walk it across the room to the managing editor, who would walk it upstairs to the publisher, who would decide whether Gus Harding would take it to Mr. William Grant. Hand Mr. Grant the story, watch him read it, and then ask the salient questions: Any comment? Is this story accurate?

And then what? the managing editor said. We know it's accurate.

We print, the publisher said.

Are you sure about that?

We are not in the business of suppressing news, the publisher said. That's not what we do. Moreover, it's an inspiring story. It's the story of a man who—triumphed over adversity. Held bad cards. Dealt himself another hand. So far's I'm concerned, the son of a gun is a hero.

The managing editor opened his mouth a fraction but did not speak. The *Press-Gazette* often suppressed news. The lawyer arrested for drunken driving and discreetly chauffeured home by a patrolman. There were eyewitnesses. The Republican committeeman photographed inside the room when the ballot boxes were unsealed. He was supervising the count, adding a stroke here and subtracting one there.

The publisher thought a moment while he lit a cigar. What does Ayres think?

Neddy is on the fence, the editor said.

Get him up here, the publisher said. We'll hash this one out right now.

Ned Ayres was out of the office. By the time he returned, the story was in galley proof with the headline "A Second Life." The publisher had determined that the piece would run on page one, below the fold, with a photograph of William Grant on the golf course. They gathered around the publisher's desk, the publisher, the managing editor, Gus Harding, and Ned Ayres. Gus Harding did volunteer the information that Fred whatever-his-name-was did not inspire confidence. An awful son of a bitch, Gus said. Not trustworthy? the publisher asked. The material checks out, Gus said. Every *i* dotted, every *t* crossed. Airtight, he added. The publisher, Carl Kaminski, turned to Ned Ayres, silent these many minutes. He was the junior man in the room by twenty years. Carl said, Do you have an opinion on these matters? For a moment Ned did not speak.

They were standing in the publisher's bare-bones office, three uncomfortable chairs, a davenport, a coffee table, a plain pine desk, and a pendulum clock in the corner that discharged a muted chime every fifteen minutes. The clock ran two hours slow and had done so for years, but its great age and scrollwork around the face commanded attention. The fifteen-minute interval suggested a quick pace, a trot, while everything else in the room was stationary. The room was spare, no photographs or artworks or citations from Kiwanis or the Elks. The single sash window looked past the department store to the Daggett River, and beyond that the golf course, where even now a foursome could be seen finishing a round. Dusk was coming on and the clock chime sounded once more. The four men were silent now, all of them considering the task at hand. We haven't really considered the effect on him and his family, Gus said. That's been settled, the publisher said. Certainly the situation was unique, the managing editor, Tom Kenny, thought but did not say. The story was serious in a way that others had not been. An important story, one with meaning, even if that meaning was elusive. Subject to interpretation. More than a story, certainly; more like a saga, something Jack London might have written or thought about. The story had grit. All the known facts were in order. The men all stood a little taller, waiting for young Ned Ayres to speak. Carl Kaminski broke the silence.

He said, Speak up, boy.

Ned was silent a moment more. He had never been asked his opinion on anything but the most routine situations. He was young and therefore inexperienced, except with the younger element in town. But he'd had no similar situations he could draw on. There were ambiguities that would be beyond him. A bright lad, yes; but brightness took you only so far. Experience in the trenches won the day. Carl had asked the question out of politeness. Ned was city editor; he could have his say along with the others. But now it seemed he was out of his depth. Well, Carl thought, this was good experience, a building block for the future. And so Carl buried his irritation and waited stolidly for what was to come.

Ned continued to stare at the pendulum clock, at a loss. He felt his eyes twitch. There seemed to him to be no cut-and-dried answer. An editor could go either way, Ned wanted to say. Let's think about this overnight. Give the story a moment to gel. But it was gelled. It was as gelled as it would ever be, one fact after another, all of them verified.

Time's wasting, Carl said.

So he would have to improvise. He had always been good at improvisation. Ned explained that he had read Gus Harding's piece with the closest attention. He believed it brought the reader a better understanding of human nature, mistakes made, mistakes redeemed or not redeemed, and the reach of plain fate in the affairs of human beings. Something inexorable about it. That would be the element of chance in a man's life. Something of the devil, too. Fred. Or, Ned went on in a rush, not sure of his ground because the publisher was looking at him in a strange way—or, to be precise, to look beyond the facts, as if the facts were a kind of, well, blindman's buff, a thicket in which one could lose one's way. Easy to be overwhelmed by them, facts, so numerous and at times contradictory. So difficult to judge motive. Was William Grant trying to put something over on them? Or was he sincere in trying to salvage his life? That is to say, bury his past, beginning with the name change. That was fundamental. He had been shamed, and now he sought to erase the shame . . . Ned's voice trailed off.

Gus Harding's piece was pristine, though clumsy in places. The clumsiness added to the authenticity. The facts ruled, but the facts did not include context. Context was beyond a reporter's brief, involving, as it did, speculation. Also, if William Grant had been a bus driver, there would be no story. It was a story because William Grant was prosperous, owned a business, married the banker's daughter, was generally admired. In its own way William Grant's story was inspiring, a cautionary tale of—what? Resilience. Ambition. More to the point, Gus's story was the truth and fortified by fact. Written without slant.

Ned said finally, Gus has done a fine job. A professional job. No mysteries here. It's dispassionate. I say print.

Carl Kaminski grunted. His eyes were on the pendulum clock. He said, There's always mystery, Ned. It is not given to us to know it all. Question is, do we know enough?

Managing editor Tom Kenny sighed and spoke for the first time. He said to Carl, Well, Chief, I'm going to have to disagree with you on that. We know what there is to know. I'm confident in the integrity—

Some facts are missing, Carl said. This is always the case, no exceptions. I hope they're no-account facts. Otherwise, we're on the wrong side of things. No criticism of you, Gus. It's the nature of our work.

I've left nothing out, Gus said. Nothing. Except Fred's bad breath. Awful.

The tension in the room eased. Carl said, What? Garlic?

I don't know, Gus said. I can find out.

Forget it, Carl said. The pendulum clock chimed. So we print, he said, and in any case, Mr. Grant will have his opportunity to rebut. If he has nothing to say, if all he offers is bluster, then we print.

The meeting broke up at six p.m. Gus Harding was instructed to show the story to William Grant. It's fair to say that none of the four newspapermen were entirely happy with the deliberations. Fred was a question mark. Unspoken among them was the near certainty that the story would be picked up on the AP wire. It would have national distribution, and the *Press-Gazette* would be under a scrutiny unknown in the paper's history. The available facts would be checked and checked again by outsiders, reporters with no knowledge of Herman beyond Ed Watts's slanders. Some of the reporters would be contemptuous of a little pissant paper to hell and gone in Indiana. Tom Kenny was of that view. The national press was remorseless, with an arrogance that had to be seen to be believed. So Herman would be on the map as something other than Joke Town. They'll tear us apart, Tom said. Ned Ayres looked at this prospect the other way around. He was interested in how the big feet danced, how they carried themselves, their interviewing techniques. Did they use tape recorders? Ned knew they traveled in packs and had no sympathy for small, isolated American towns of the sort described by Sinclair Lewis. Theodore Dreiser. Still, Ned imagined that for a short period of time William Grant Haberdashery would be as familiar to the world as Marshall Field & Co. He couldn't wait.

The slant of the piece was undeniably sympathetic to William Grant, a man who had remade himself. He had owed a debt to society and had settled the debt. He had gone straight. Gus had spoken to William Grant's lawyer, who confirmed that his fantasist defense was weak, in the circumstances ill advised. Not that it wasn't true. That was exactly Grant's profile. No question, he lived in a dreamworld. But alas, fantasy did not trump breaking and entering, robbery, and assault. And Grant's surly demeanor worked against him, his scarred face, his great height. He frightened the jury. His decision to invoke the Fifth Amendment won him suspicion, not sympathy. I've worried this case for many years, the lawyer said. But it was the only defense I had. Billy was certainly guilty. Beyond a doubt. But still . . . The lawyer's voice trailed off. A soft click indicated he had ended the conversation.

That left William Grant. Gus arrived at the haberdashery at nine the next morning. As he expected, the hour was too early for customers. Grant was in the rear of the store checking the display of suits, the latest offerings from Hart, Schaffner & Marx, heavy serge suits for the winter soon to come. Gus waited a moment in the front of the store, then walked to the rear and introduced himself. If Mr. Grant had a few moments, Gus had a newspaper article the paper intended to run the next day. He would like a comment, if Mr. Grant chose to give one.

In the sharp fluorescence of the store, Gus noted an oily patina on William Grant's furrowed face, a kind of conditioner that had sheen to it. William Grant said, What's it all about? Gus handed him the galley proof, and at first glance Grant's eyes closed and his hands went to his ravaged face. The galley proof floated to the floor. Gus Harding picked it up and handed it to him once more. William Grant murmured something unintelligible and commenced to read the proof. His face was tight, strange with its sheen. He read slowly while Gus waited. When he finished, a rough look came to him, the look of a prizefighter in his corner before the bell. Some arrogance there, Gus thought, the way Grant spoke, a clipped speech. What's it's all about? He was nicely turned out in a blue blazer and gray flannel slacks, a blood-red Jack London at his throat. He took a step forward, crowding Gus. Gus slid his notebook from his pocket, a pen already in his hand. Show the colors, he thought. The haberdasher glared at the reporter as if he were a ghost-messenger, someone from an infernal place, scarcely human. But when he spoke, his voice was temperate.

William Grant said, Please do not print this.

Gus Harding said, Is it inaccurate? If it is, I can fix that.

It is not inaccurate.

Gus made a note on his pad.

I beg you not to print this. This—filth.

We think it is an inspiring story. The publisher himself said so.

It will not be inspiring to my family. My family will fall apart. Once they see it—

They will not see it. I will not allow it.

Mr. Grant—

My family does not know. They know nothing of my life when I was young.

I see, Gus said.

No, you do not see. William Grant took a step forward, his hands, now fists, rigid at his side. He said, I have a settled life here. I have done no one harm. I run my business and take care of my family. I have a wife, two sons. I love those boys more than I can say. What right do you have—

There are court records, Gus said. In the public domain. I have spoken to your lawyer, who gave me a sympathetic account—

—to interfere.

Gus made another note on his pad.

What do you want? Do you want money? I can give you money.

Mr. Grant!

As for your records. They are public when you choose to make them public. This is your decision.

Please look at my article again, Mr. Grant. It is not an unsympathetic story. It describes a man—and then Gus remembered the publisher's words. A man who dealt himself a fresh hand. A man determined to succeed in the world. A man determined to put his unfortunate past behind him. Really, a triumph.

I will be ruined, Grant said. My wife will be ruined. My wife, my children. They will be ruined also if you print this garbage.

It is not garbage. My story has been verified.

It is not your story. It is my story.

It is in the public domain, Gus said. Would you like to speak to my publisher?

I am speaking to you. You who have taken my life and written it up. You wrote it and you must take responsibility for it.

Yes, Gus began.

I have worked so hard—

And been successful. Very successful. The object of envy. And your offense was years back. No one remembers.

Yes, that's the point. Don't you see?

Gus made another note on his pad.

What are you writing? Stop writing! I have not given you permission to write. Stop it at once. William Grant turned away, his hand resting on the shoulder of a mannequin dressed in a Hart, Schaffner & Marx blue serge suit. The haberdasher fingered the cloth as if testing its durability, how it would wear in the bitter cold of an Indiana January. Gus noticed again the sheen on his cheeks and forehead. William Grant was perspiring heavily. He seemed to think that the newspaper had no rights in the matter. Everyone had a life that must be owned up to. That was the point Grant could not escape. He had made mistakes and paid for the mistakes, but that did not make the mistakes go away. It was hard to understand. Here he was, being offered a clean bill of health over three columns on page one with a photograph, and he was insulted by it. Gus made another note on his pad, though Grant did not notice this because he was looking out the window. A passerby waved and Grant waved back.

Gus cleared his throat but said nothing. They seemed at an

impasse. Well and good. Point was, the public interest came first. That meant the public's right to know, and that was what Mr. William Grant would not concede. Even so, Gus Harding felt sorry for the haberdasher whose troubled voice gave away so much.

Is this your business, ruining people?

I don't see it that way, Gus said.

Because that's the consequence.

William Grant let the blue serge slip from his fingers and the suit coat dropped to the floor. He sighed heavily, in other circumstances a signal that he was ill.

I'm only doing my job, Gus said.

Grant looked up and gave a crooked smile, sarcastic around the edges. He said, Is that right?

That's right. That's what I do.

Still smiling, Grant said, I suppose you let the chips fall where they may.

That's it, Gus said.

There's no escaping you people, Grant said. Scavengers. That's what you are, scavengers of dirty linen. And you call that serving the public interest.

Gus made another note on his pad.

Stop that! Grant said.

Gus looked up from his notepad.

Where'd you find this story? Who told you about it?

I had a source, Gus said.

Does this source have a name? Or wouldn't that serve your public interest.

Gus thought a moment, then decided to break the rule. He said, Your friend Fred.

Fred who? I don't know any Fred.

He wouldn't give up his last name.

Describe him.

Heavyset, thick goatee. He had a tattoo on his arm. Maybe he was fifty or so.

William Grant shook his head. And this Fred called you?

We met out of town, Gus said.

William Grant seemed to sag slightly. His hands went to his face, touching the scars. He said, I don't know who that can be. He accused me. I don't even know his name and neither do you. He paused again, staring out the window onto Benjamin Franklin Boulevard. He said in a low voice, Get the hell out of my store, Harding. Don't come back.

Gus closed his notebook and put it in his pocket. He said, Thank you for your time, Mr. Grant. I'll leave you these, he added, placing the newspaper articles, the court transcripts, and the rest on the table that displayed tie pins, shirt studs, and handkerchiefs. William Grant said nothing. Gus said, For what it's worth, I don't think Fred was his real name. And he is a lowlife. But that does not mean his story is not genuine.

And in a moment Gus Harding was out the door and on the sidewalk in a gray drizzle. He lit a cigarette and stood, ill at ease, looking in the haberdasher's window, suits and shirts, Bass Weejun loafers, socks of various lengths and colors, suspenders, even a silver-handled ebony umbrella with a little printed card: Not For Sale. When Gus looked inside the store, William Grant stared back at him, a look of the most profound confusion. Hatred was there, too, and sorrow. The blue serge suit coat was still gathered at his feet. With infinite patience William Grant bent to retrieve the coat and replaced it on its plastic hanger.

Leatrice Grant had no idea of her husband's wretched past. He had told her he had been in the navy, hence the scars on his face. Not a childhood accident at all but the result of a mission on navy business. She must never speak of it. The mission was highly classified. That evening was an evening like any other, except that William was unusually quiet. He put the children to bed and read them a story amid squeals of laughter. He and Leatrice watched television until ten, then went to bed themselves. Leatrice had the idea they might fool around a little, her demure reference to sex. But William was reluctant. He was, as he said, bushed, a refusal most unlike him. But he came around as he always did, a little rough at the end but Leatrice with her rangy body liked that. He fell asleep at once while she lingered for a while. The next morning, Leatrice woke late. Her husband had left the bedroom early, had showered and shaved, and returned to kiss his wife goodbye and said softly that he loved her very much, what he always said when he left the house to go to work. Leatrice smiled and slept on. She herself had a hair appointment at ten. William would see to the children.

When Leatrice opened the garage door she saw her husband hanging in the shadows of the top rafter, naked except for undershorts. His face was bloated, eyes wide open in a death stare, and for the briefest moment she did not recognize him. Then she took a step back, unwilling to believe what was in front of her eyes. Then she screamed, a long, loud wail of anguish and horror. She pitched to the floor of the garage and there she remained until the neighbors, alarmed at what they heard through the open garage door, came slowly to the driveway to find Leatrice and then William. For the longest time no one moved, the neighbors stricken, frozen in place in a kind of pantomime. It took a minute or two before someone called the police. Who would volunteer to collect David and Eugene at school? Their grandfather, of course. He must be told at once, and a doctor to see to poor Leatrice. Several of the women gathered up Leatrice and helped her inside the house. She had lost control of her limbs and did not speak. Her eyes were closed.

The note was soon discovered and handed discreetly to Leatrice's father when he arrived. The note said, Fuck You All. There was no signature. Howard Elias put the note in his pocket without reading it and did not appear to understand what it was. At last a friend told him that the boys should be picked up at school and volunteered to drive Howard the few blocks. Howard agreed, but only after he had seen his daughter. He stepped inside the house and closed the door. By that time the early edition of the *Press-Gazette* was on the street, the distinctive green trucks all over downtown Herman. "A Second Life" was displayed on page one, above the fold. No one could miss it. Later that day, Howard Elias read Grant's note and tore it to pieces.

The weeks following William Grant's death were an ordeal. Reporters from as far away as Los Angeles and London arrived to cover the story, so dense with nuance and irony, and mystery also. The out-of-town reporters were brash and soon learned that Leatrice and her boys were staying with relatives in Chicago, and so a part of the pack sped north, laying siege to a brownstone near the Edgewater Beach Hotel, said to be the family's place of refuge. However, the siege failed: Leatrice refused to show her face, and indeed some doubted that she and the boys were in Chicago at all, and so in time the reporters returned to Herman.

In two weeks, Leatrice and her boys returned to Herman for the delayed burial of William Grant, held at a late hour and lasting a bare fifteen minutes. There were no eulogies, only the reading of a single psalm followed by ten minutes of silence. The press was kept at a distance, cordoned off from the ceremony until the family had departed. Ned Ayres found himself surrounded, asked to identify the mourners, and Ned obliged, pointing out the mayor and the city treasurer, the police chief and the principal of the high school, all in dark suits. Ned omitted mention of his father the judge, who was in a foul mood that day. Ned thought it a charade, his impromptu briefing, a session with the most senior correspondents flown in for the occasion, including three television newsreaders with their impedimenta, cameramen and soundmen with their heavy cameras and glaring lights; it was early days in the television trade, the newsreaders ill at ease owing to the nature of the story, its grisly aspect, its pathos. Children might be listening in. The townspeople looked on aghast. Couldn't these outsiders wait a decent interval? Everyone was moving now, the mourners holding umbrellas in the light rain that had just begun to fall, the reporters attempting interviews, most of the attempts unsuccessful. The mourners were both appalled and mystified by the hostile army that had insinuated itself into their private grief. Uncle Ralph had stood a little apart, but now he turned and pointed his umbrella at the assembled press. We know who you are! he cried. You are welcome to join us, you and your men, he said, nodding at a British correspondent, the tall one in a trench coat, the one with military bearing. In different circumstances Judge Ayres would have restrained his brother, but on this occasion he did nothing. When the cameras turned toward him, Uncle Ralph appeared to have a fit, his arms flailing, spittle flying from his mouth. The judge moved to put his arms around his brother but Uncle Ralph broke free and soon enough was on the ground entangled in the umbrella. The cameras moved elsewhere, searching for the widow and her children. But Leatrice and the boys had slipped away quietly, surrounded by friends. In the end all that remained was the freshly dug grave with its naked cross, the name and the name's dates yet to be carved. Ned remained there a while, the press having moved off in a pack, the mourners dispersing, the rain continuing to fall.

That night the judge said to his son, You're in a nasty business. Corrupt at its heart. A jury of voyeurs. Don't you think?

They're people doing a job, Ned said, and left the room.

Ned Ayres's curiosity was focused on the pencil press, the inquiring faces and piercing eyes, a notebook always near to hand. They carried themselves with authority, most of them, a necessary part of the democratic process, meaning any event with national reach. They were especially interested in the lore and legends of Herman. What made Herman tick? What did people do for amusement? The most dogged was a Boston reporter named Finn, barely five and a half feet tall, tousled hair, freckles, always laughing—when he was not at the ball diamond, the tennis court, the golf course, the pool table, or the pool, a scratch player in all sports. He resembled one of Norman Rockwell's *Saturday Evening Post* mischievous kids and therefore not highly valued by the other reporters. A rascal. Not serious. Drank sparingly. Finn happily spent time with Ned, urging him not to remain an editor. A terrible idea. Don't do it. Don't be an inside man, the road to nowhere. A mouse in training to become a rat.

At night the press corps gathered at a bar in Mill City. They were motley, some dressed like safari guides, others like bankers. Among them were the indisputably senior men and a few women of wide experience, their work dating back to the Battle of the Somme and the Coolidge administration, Omaha Beach and the McCarthy hysteria. One of them had interviewed F. Scott Fitzgerald in Paris. Ned Ayres was enthralled by their adventures, always well told; they were wonderful raconteurs, especially the two who had been at the Somme. They were now in their seventies, trim men who wore bow ties and fedoras, their scotch taken neat. To them the Herman story was a rollover, signifying nothing much beyond misfortune. Most everyone agreed that they would not be long in Indiana because the Grant story did not have legs. It was a story good for a month, perhaps two months. In time the widow would be found and interrogated. She would wish to tell her story. That would be the definitive end of the saga, if saga it was. Well, saga would be the wrong word. Tragedy, too, seemed lofty. The Grant story was easily told, a man who wanted another identity, one that would allow him to live like an ordinary person. The revanchist Fred put an end to it—and there you had it. Fred plus a naïve provincial editor was a toxic mix. But that did not add up to legs. It added up to Mr. Nobody from Nowhere, a man who, push came to shove, could not take the heat. His dream was all he had, and when the dream collapsed, so did the haberdasher. And so the reporters drifted away from Herman, and in three weeks they were all gone.

Ned Ayres missed their company. They were resilient. They knew the world or at least that part of it deemed famous or notorious or anyhow humanly interesting. They knew the man who bit the dog, the pigeon who lived among the cats. They were good company, people you'd want around the dinner table. Never a dull moment, and the truth of the matter was that accidental victims slipped out of the news as easily as they slipped into it, and in that way the caravan moved on. Of course the reporters were bored in Herman. And Herman was fed up with them. However, the story did not die as neatly as predicted. It nagged at people like a loose tooth. It had legs after all.

In Indianapolis and later in Muncie and finally in Detroit, Leatrice found time to change her name and the names of her children from Grant to Kelly. Twice she returned to Herman for the funerals of her parents. At those times she visited the grave of her husband, standing alone in midafternoon, once in November, four years later in October, both days bright with sunlight. She was so heavily veiled it was impossible to inspect her face. In the event, the cemetery was deserted except for two gravediggers leaning on their shovels some distance away. If Leatrice noticed the litter near her husband's grave, she said nothing about it.

The fascination with the death of William Grant went on for some time, turning naturally to the responsibilities of the *Press-Gazette*. Had the ethics of journalism been violated? And by the way, what precisely were those ethics? There were symposia aplenty in journalism schools around the country and, as might be expected, in the nation's newsrooms. One of the newsmagazines put the story on its cover, breaking tradition to assign the piece to a much-admired British novelist. The piece was elegantly done, observing that error was inherent in any human activity, no exceptions. But the problem was not factual error. Should the story have been published at all? Did the dead have rights? Did a family have rights? Conundrums all. In the end there was a sort of consensus: whatever the faults, feints, and missteps of the nation's press in general and the Herman newspaper in particular, William Grant had supervised his own fate, wrote the note, strung the noose. Certainly there was tremendous sympathy for the survivors, his wife and his sons. What had they done to deserve this? A fresh expression of military origin found its way into the vocabulary of the newspapers: "collateral damage." Leatrice, David, and Eugene were collateral damage. "Deserve" didn't come into it. An icy formulation, Ned Ayres thought, responsibility as an afterthought, including a gap in the agreed-upon version of events. No one knew what William Grant thought or did between the time he slipped from his bedroom and, then or later, found himself in his garage with a length of rope in his hand, paper and pencil nearby. What was in his mind was unknown. A note was known to exist, but no one had read it. Its whereabouts were unknown. So the thing was a mystery. Without the note there would always be an unanswered question. Suicide was so often an act of defiance. The British polymath brought chaos theory into play. A hateful father, a prison term, a badly wired conscience, and years later a suicide in Herman.

Two seasons later polls showed that the reading public had lost interest. William Grant was deemed a loser. The story moved from page one to the inside, articles of a few hundred words, and then to the news briefs, and finally—silence. The newspapers were deprived of facts. There was nothing new. Ned was reminded of the cuspidor that rested beside the obit desk, a droll comment on the last curtain call. It had been there for many years. It was thought that the tap of a shoe on the cuspidor would bring luck. *Ding!* Ned Ayres wondered if William Grant was the toe or the cuspidor and concluded he was both. But then, in his most private thoughts, Ned deemed himself to have a hard heart. He thought that the news business forced that, the discovering of secrets with little attention paid to the consequences. Ned Ayres remembered also the old adage. The first version was always wrong, if only slightly.

After his rendezvous with Michael Ardmore those many years ago, Ned remembered his long trek down Michigan Avenue ending at the roiling waters of the Chicago River. The time was near midnight. His eyelids were frozen from the cold. He had been so deep in his memory that he had forgotten where he was. This was long after William Grant's death. He had been drinking with Michael at his club, Michael so torn apart by his daughter's death that he had to excuse himself. He had lost his composure, and when he returned they talked about the news business, to no grand conclusion. Michael was a skeptic. His heart was not in it. Well, he too was gone now. He seemed not to have had the will to find his daughter's grave, assuming the grave could be located. Probably it could. Ned Ayres remembered thinking that it was good to be a loner in the news business. The business had a way of taking over. Nothing was so dire that a wisecrack couldn't loosen it, make it visible, bring it home, whatever it was. Always one had to be scrupulous as to time and place, the facts. Suppositions were verboten. Take nothing for granted. When Kennedy was killed, schoolchildren in Dallas cheered.

Ned remembered being chilled all the way through. His office was only a few yards away so he thought to pay it a visit, see if there was anything new on the wires. He used his keys to open the big brass entrance door and the narrower inner door behind it. He had the sensation of going home, a *querencia* where he would find safety from skeptics. His apartment could be lonely and the newsroom was never lonely, especially when it was empty. It was a refuge. The building's foyer was a kind of echo chamber, the walls decorated with celebrated front pages. The end of the Second World War. The beginning of the Civil War. The opening of the transcontinental railway and one or two ludicrous ones to show that the management could take a joke. The morning paper had long before been put to bed. He remembered the bottle of scotch in his office credenza. He rode the empty elevator to the empty newsroom, fetched the bottle, and poured a half glass, all the while looking at the empty desks that seemed to go on forever, each identical. The wire machines were chattering but he paid no attention. Instead, he sat in his swivel chair and put his feet on the desk. Ned Ayres sipped whiskey and read an unpublished piece marked for his attention. It was lengthy, fifty inches or more, a botched attempt describing the widow Jacqueline Kennedy's romantic adventures. The piece was beyond salvage, a farrago of conjecture and magical thinking thinly fortified by anonymous quotations ripe with innuendo. The writer had fashioned a cartoon. Ned wrote a note in the margin ending with "See me." He straightened the papers on his desk, then put them away in the top drawer and locked the drawer. He straightened the framed photographs on the credenza, his father and mother in their youth, leaning on golf sticks at the Daggett Golf Club, a sunny afternoon in golden October before the Grant troubles. There was a snapshot of Elaine in her black bikini. Next to the snapshot was a marble bust of the ravaged face of Homer, he whose faith in the whims of the gods was near absolute. He liked Homer's unsentimental view of Achilles: "The most violent man in the world." Homer was a storyteller, nothing more. He was not a moral conscience. But what a storyteller!

Ned sipped whiskey, lit a cigarette, and stepped into the newsroom. He had come to love it as if it belonged to him, an old clock that kept perfect time. He knew every desk and every man and woman behind every desk. He thought there was nothing so replete as an abandoned newsroom in the very early morning. Something immaculate about it, its raw potential, a slack tide, the boat adrift, sails close-hauled. God alone knew what mischief awaited. A celebrity dead of an overdose, the skull of a dinosaur discovered in North Dakota, a 250-pound RAF bomb discovered in a Rotterdam sewer, a souvenir of War Two. Ned stood still as a deer in the headlights. He remembered the crush of reporters arriving in Herman after the Grant suicide, asking questions of everyone they met. Herman had never seen anything like it. People did not know how to answer the questions, so brusquely put, questions that demanded answers. What exactly did these out-of-town people want to know? They tried to turn away but the reporters turned with them. How do you feel about all this? This death. What was he like, this Grant? And so, lacking coherent thoughts of their own, the townspeople, without quite realizing what they were doing, answered the way people did in such circumstances, imitated what they had seen and heard on television. They were a lovely couple. A fine pair of sons. Not active in the community, no. They were— just a family, trying to get on like the rest of us. Ned Ayres was the front man in the absence of Gus Harding, who was undone and had taken a fortnight's leave. And not too long after that the rumors gathered. The communists were somehow involved, the hanging of William Grant not a hanging at all but a lynching. The paper's trying to cover it up. The clues were manipulated by the authorities and the ghouls of the *Press-Gazette*. Ned thought that of those directly involved, Gus Harding was the one with the clearest conscience. His article was entirely straightforward, a professional job, spare sentences, the facts allowed to carry the story. It was not an eloquent piece. In fact it was laconic, almost mundane, free of sentimentality and yet sympathetic. Friends told Harding that if his subject had read it, he would not have taken his own life, never in a million years. But that was not the way Gus saw it. He thought of himself as an accomplice to an avoidable tragedy, his assembly of facts in disarray, without discipline. He couldn't remember the last time he had a bad conscience but he had one now. He had allowed William Grant to get under his skin. That was Gus's private worry. He had not probed deeply enough into Grant's past. He had not given context to the story of the appalling Fred. The one accusation that Gus discarded was Fred's fairy business, surely false. He told no one of it, not even his wife. He felt good about that, especially the following afternoon when he was obliged to write the second-day story that ran on page one, below the fold this time, half the length of "A Second Life." Ned Ayres was told to edit, a demanding chore because Gus's piece was disheveled. It was unprintable until finally Gus gave it up and marched from the newsroom, head down. In the event, the second-day story carried no byline. Gus had insisted on that.

A few months later Gus Harding took early retirement and moved to Muncie to be near his grown children. Three evenings a week he filled in on the copy desk of the Muncie paper. Quiet work: putting the commas in the right places, checking the spelling, eliminating flights of fancy, four-syllable words, and unsubstantiated facts. That Gus, the city editor said, he's a treasure.

Ned Ayres followed Gus Harding. The day before he was to leave Herman for Indianapolis he took a walk around town, one end of Benjamin Franklin Boulevard and back again. He walked in soft sunlight, a lovely September day, a natural masterpiece with no hint of the winter soon to come. Elms in full leaf leaned across the boulevard in an arbor, and for a moment Ned thought of a foreign land, provincial France or the hill towns of Tuscany. He had become acquainted with both in his European civilization class in the twelfth grade. He admired these towns from a distance, so old, ancient really, thick with tradition, from the outside most peaceful. By contrast, Herman was only brick and mortar. It had been settled before the Civil War but no buildings, neither stores nor houses, survived from that time. Ned was entranced by the idea of France and Italy, but it never occurred to him that he might visit there himself. Instead, he had Indianapolis. He was twenty-one years old now with a manner older than his age, no doubt a consequence of his decision to avoid college life with its frivolity, its fads and lonely passions, its conformity. He had been working after hours since he was fourteen and full-time at the *Post-Gazette* since graduation from high school, honors all around. Herman had become a straitjacket but he knew he would miss it, if only as a measuring stick. Herman was a place he had left but a half-dozen times in his life, two field trips to Chicago — the Museum of Science and Industry in the morning, the Art Institute in the afternoon — and trips with his family to Louisville and east to Kenyon, in Ohio. His father was insistent about college and had heard nice things about Kenyon and its English Department. Judge Ayres knew that Indiana University, his old school, was not suitable. Too large and rah-rah and at the same time confined, landlocked. But Ned refused even to entertain the idea of higher education. His father made the application to Kenyon anyhow, and when the acceptance came, Ned refused to open the letter. He knew what he would do with his working life and college was a distraction, yesterday's news. Something would be lost, certainly, but much more would be gained because Ned would be submerged in the news. The rest he could pick up as he went along. Shakespeare and Carnegie and Picasso and Newton and Homer, even Big Bill Thompson, Chicago's crooked mayor between the wars, and Indiana's flirtation with the Ku Klux Klan. The Battle of the Somme. Ned believed he had successfully managed the first stage of his apprenticeship. Indianapolis was the next stage, and then — who knew? He thought of Chicago.

Ned strolled by the Buick dealership and the pharmacy, the coffee shop next to the pharmacy. He waved to old Mr. Neggin and old Mr. Neggin waved back before returning to his urn. Ned thought of stopping in to see Uncle Ralph, then decided not to. The old soldier slept most of the day and night, and even when he was awake he was silent except for an occasional nonsense sentence. His hands were restless and now and again he whistled a tune from the Great War, looking at his steepled thumbs. The judge continued to stop in on Saturday mornings, stay five minutes, and leave. Ned passed the courthouse where his father was in the discovery phase of a trial, something to do with bankruptcy. Ned glanced at the window of Johnson's Jewelry and its spread of Bulova wristwatches and engagement rings. Then he was at the window of William Grant Haberdashery with its hand-lettered For Sale sign with the telephone number of the bank. The interior was empty, dust on the floor, an electric wire hanging naked where an overhead light had been. Ned shook his head at the disarray. William Grant had always been tidy, racks of double-breasted blue suits, racks of ties and display cases of shirts and sweaters, ribbed black socks, red suspenders. Ned remembered the umbrella with its ebony staff and silver handle with its discreet notice: Not For Sale. As if any man in Herman would buy such an accessory. Whatever did Grant have in mind? The ebony reflected a soft glow, suitable for a slender dancer in a top hat and a white silk scarf, wingtip shoes, a lime-colored shirt with French cuffs and little blue initials over the breast pocket, and a silk vest with a gold chain that went across the waist from here to there. Poor Grant, he thought he was bringing a touch of class to worn-out Herman. So the lawyer was correct after all. The haberdasher was, first and last, a fantasist.

All this and more tumbled from Ned's memory as he stood at his desk in the newsroom on Michigan Avenue in Chicago waiting for the next act. The time was past midnight. He returned the bottle of scotch to its place in the credenza. He made no move to leave, his eyes patrolling the great vacant room. The card players had vanished. The night watchman looked in, gave a wave, and continued on. Ned smiled, thinking it was time for him to move from the middle of the country to its eastern edge. There were different lessons to learn in the East, an older environment with still a ways to go. In the East things were less confined because of the open ocean and settlements that dated from the sixteenth century, all in all a more forgiving ambiance—and then Salem and the witch-hunts came to mind. Well. He would have to see for himself, and Washington was a good place to begin.

Later in that dreadful year, Ned's last in Herman, someone had the temerity to put the *Post-Gazette* up for a Pulitzer Prize, the gold medal for public service, the idea being to show support for the nation's newspapers, beleaguered but courageous as ever. The nation's provincial press deserved words of encouragement. A vigilant watchman of the night. But the nomination did not survive the first cut. The Grant story had slipped off the screen, too much attention paid to it and so many loose ends. Too much inside chatter. Very many questions without satisfactory answers. Just about everyone was happy to see it disappear, including Ned Ayres. The story began as something instructive and ended in rancor and confusion. Ned turned off his office light and stood in the near darkness. He lit a cigarette, thinking of Elaine, thinking too of Michael Ardmore, who was his own verification. Elaine went her own way, so did her father. Thing was, you could never leave the business altogether. The business was truly a kind of cult, and difficult to read your own motives because your work was the full disclosure of the motives of others. That was the way the board was set up, the dice in play. Looked at in a certain way, the way of utter neutrality—well, William Grant didn't stand a chance.

Ned Ayres buttoned his coat and took one last look around. He hurried through the newsroom until he reached the bank of elevators.

In twenty minutes Ned was home, switching on lights as he went from room to room. His feet hurt. He wondered if another glass of scotch would brighten the evening and decided it would not. He stood at the picture window looking into dimly lit and empty Astor Street. God, that was an awful piece about Jacqueline Kennedy. He wondered how much of it was factual. Probably not much. The younger reporters took liberties that the older ones did not, as if the typewriter keys were little magic wands that conferred reliability, the machine a kind of god. Maybe there should be an age requirement in the newsroom, say thirty years old, men and women alike. Let them learn their trade on a smaller paper where the stakes weren't so high and an old-timer could warn them about adverbs, and not in a kindly way. A bark with an expletive at the end of it showing that he meant business. Well, the stakes were often high on smaller papers, too. Ned continued to look out the window at the single streetlight and a couple necking, pressed against the chassis of a blue Cadillac as the snow commenced to fall.

Sometime in the early morning Ned awoke in a state of high confusion. He had been dreaming or hallucinating, one or the other. He was in a dark place, a city park or private lawn. He lay still, allowing things to settle. His memory stretched back. He was speaking to old man Elias, his family scattered, his life in ruins. His wife was ill. The bank was up for sale. He rarely heard from Leatrice and the boys. At Christmastime he sent them checks but the notes that came back were pro forma, a Hallmark card with a scribble on its face. Ned Ayres sat up in bed. The hallucination vanished and he returned to real time, three a.m. according to the clock on the bedside table. The encounter had come at dusk on the day before Ned was to leave for Indianapolis. Ned had seen Mr. Elias accept the note, look at it, and tear it into pieces. He had never told anyone, figuring that the Grant matter should have one inviolable secret. There had been the usual rumors about the note that Grant had left behind. No one had seen it except his father-in-law; seen and destroyed. Ned told him that he was leaving town, probably for good. They spoke briefly about the old man's family, and Ned made the inquiry. What had the note said? He realized at once that he had crossed a line. He apologized. Forget it, he said. I'm sorry I asked. Howard Elias turned away without speaking. Ned left the question hanging. The old man sighed, as much groan as sigh. He seemed to be gathering himself from some unspeakable burden.

What did you say?

I'm sorry. I asked about Grant's farewell note.

Oh, Howard Elias said. It was a short note.

Ned said, The missing element.

Howard Elias offered a thin smile, as one does on contemplating a simple answer to a complex question.

He looked at Ned, then lowered his voice. William said he was sorry for the trouble he had caused. "I am so very sorry," William wrote. It was a gentleman's note, you see. Unsigned, but I recognized the script, Howard said.

Five

MILO PASSAREL

ONCE A FORTNIGHT Ned Ayres dined with the publisher of the newspaper. They met at the publisher's downtown club, usually at the table in the far corner of the room, the one with the glancing view of the fortified gates of the White House, the mansion white-lit beyond. That evening, a little after eight, they met in the bar but decided to go directly to the dining room, the bar being crowded with noisy lawyers. Their language was filthy, even the women. Milo Passarel was a gentleman of the old school, as people liked to say, courteous almost to a fault. He was often silent and always booked the table known as the Coolidge table, in memory of Silent Cal, who once spent an entire evening mute as a stone. So inconspicuous was the president that one evening he disappeared into the gents and when next seen was strolling across Lafayette Square and up the driveway to his house, where he knocked on the door and was admitted by a Marine guard who saluted and asked for ID. That, anyhow, was the story.

Milo, like President Coolidge, was easy to underestimate, mildly spoken and abrupt without being contentious, perhaps miscast as the publisher of a newspaper, a business that was, after all, loquacious, a rumble-tumble side-of-the-mouth business that attracted more than its share of rogues and exhibitionists, skeptics, wiseguys devoted to transforming any silk purse into a sow's ear. The noisy lawyers reminded Milo of the newsroom at deadline time, not that he devoted much time to the newsroom. That was Ned Ayres's chore. And so the publisher listened a moment before escorting Ned out of the bar and into the cathedral atmosphere of the dining room, sparsely filled, two candles burning at Silent Cal's table. Milo nodded at a senator he knew slightly. Then a waitress was at their table asking for drink orders and Milo Passarel selected a bottle of Rioja, as he usually did.

I like the Rioja, Milo said. It's good value. It's low end of the scale compared to what they've got in the cellar, Chambertin and some of the really good Bordeaux, Lafitte and the others. But I prefer the Rioja, tasty, no nonsense. Built to last. They know what they're doing in Spain.

Good value, Ned replied.

Without preamble Milo Passarel began to speak of an old friend, dead of a stroke two days earlier. His obituary was in the paper that morning, an account that featured a scandal of years past, a minor scandal as Washington scandals went, but a scandal nonetheless. Placed high up in the obituary, third paragraph actually. Was that necessary, Ned? He was a good man. The obit roughed him up.

Yes, Ned said. We call it the sweet and sour balance.

More sour than sweet, the publisher said.

Ned Ayres waited a moment before replying. He said, Point taken.

People are not saints, the publisher said.

Definitely, Ned replied.

God help you in this town if you put a foot wrong.

The Justice Department was involved, Ned said.

And when his wife called me she was in tears.

Ned Ayres nodded in sympathy.

I sent your reporter a note about it. Sharply written note.

She told me, Ned said. Showed me your note. Said she wanted to speak to you, explain her method. I told her that was a bad idea. But she said her feelings were hurt and she wanted to explain why she wrote it the way she did, the sweet and sour balance. I said that was definitely a bad idea because the publisher has nothing to do with the preparation of obits. I do. I supervise obits and whatever else is in the paper. The weather report. The Dow Jones Industrial Average. Milo? Can I suggest that this obituary is way below your pay grade?

Milo raised his eyebrows and said, Nothing in the paper is below my pay grade, alas. That's why I carry the title of publisher. And it bothers me that the worst is always the first in our obituaries.

But you see what I'm saying.

Of course. That doesn't mean I approve.

The waitress arrived with the Rioja and poured without ceremony. She was young and very pretty, no doubt a substitute. Waitresses at the club were older women, blunt-spoken. This one was smiling. She deftly moved her fingernail to catch a stray drop from the bottle and glided away. Milo had seen none of this. He sighed deeply and looked out the window at the White House lawn, blue in the glare of the lights. Milo was obviously preoccupied, something beyond obituaries. Obituaries were an hors d'oeuvre. Ned had learned to remain silent at such moments. Milo Passarel's cards were always held close to the vest. His expression was unreadable, his eyes fixed on a distant point.

Milo took one wee sip of Rioja as if it were nitroglycerine and still his mien was inscrutable, a stranger at his own table. He had taken leave, gone away somewhere. He had said to Ned only the other day that he felt like an instructor who taught the same course year after year. One might say—nothing learned, nothing forgotten. He lived in his own world, no question of that, and his world was abstract. When his day ended, at precisely four forty-five in the afternoon, Milo Passarel went home and read in his library. He never worked on weekends. He was never to be disturbed except in the event of an emergency, an explosion in the building, for example. His own cast of mind was not ideal for the publisher of a newspaper. He did not relish conflict. Mischief did not interest him. An ideal page one would be repetitive, like the skin of a great ocean, no wind, no tide, a blanket of water on which no vessels were visible. A good day would be a day without obituaries. A fine day would feature a new invention, something to improve the lives of people. But his family owned the newspaper. He was the inheritor, like it or not. And so he shouldered the burden because that was what he was born to do. That was his assignment. Early in their collaboration Ned made a mistake that he never forgot and that made him laugh whenever he thought of it. He referred to the news business as "fun."

Milo said, What?

Fun, Milo. The business is fun.

You mean, like play?

Well, not play exactly. More in the line of The Human Comedy.

Milo grunted.

You don't agree?

It's an invitation to a beheading, Milo said, a strange remark that Ned Ayres identified as a Nabokov title. And now, in the low quiet of the dining room, Milo Passarel cleared his throat, took a mouthful of Rioja, and told a story from his own life, something he almost never did. His voice dropped an octave and his eyes moved away to fasten once more on the blue lawn of the White House. He said, When I was a boy, Father allowed me to sit in on editorial conferences. I was very young. I was under ten, so much of what was said I did not catch. But I do remember the rough laughter, four or five of them, my father leading. On this one occasion they were trying to fix a plank in the party platform. The convention was a week away. The platform had gained quite a lot of attention, though everyone knew it would be utterly and completely forgotten once the convention ended and a nominee selected. They were divvying up the responsibilities. My father would write two editorials, the first conciliatory, the second not. Senator X would handle the Florida delegation. Governor Y would handle Illinois. Their voices fell as they struggled with the emissary to Eleanor. Eleanor Roosevelt was critical to their efforts. Lose Eleanor and you might lose New York. That was the consensus except for my father, who said Eleanor had but one vote in her handbag, her own. Forget Eleanor. I was half listening. I knew some of the names because they were politicians and they were the people my father, the publisher of this newspaper, socialized with. His sword was the editorial page of the paper. He cared for little else, but now and then he would arrive in the newsroom with a story of his own. He'd point with his finger and the chief political reporter would rise and they would both head for my father's office on the seventh floor. And the very next day there would be an exclusive report on page one, citing reliable sources. That was Father's life, Milo said, my grandfather's, too. That's why they owned a newspaper instead of an automobile company or a law firm. I remember them still in my father's office, all of them with a drink in hand. This was where the business got done. No stenographer, no tape recorder. The conferences were off-book. And that's how things got done. And by the way, the business of the newspaper was in other hands. We had a general manager who ran things, a report every Friday to my father, who listened carefully without actually understanding what he was told. He put up a bold front, though, as they went through the various departments, classified and circulation and distribution and the others. Father did enjoy the rumble of the presses as they began the run, and the whine when the machines were at full throat. The entire building shook, including my father's office. He never bothered with the minor departments. They were a faceless infantry forever in the trenches, remembered with a bonus check at the end of the year. Thank you for your service. Fact was, we were making so damned much money that it didn't matter.

Milo said, That's my first memory of the newspaper business.

Ned Ayres said, You should write a memoir.

Ned, sometimes you surprise me. Whatever would I want to do that for?

A tiny peek behind the scenes, Ned said. What do you call it? The Chinese screen?

Venetian blind is more like it, Milo said.

Even so, Ned said.

So that's one story of growing up in the newspaper business. Does it sound like a business to you? Not to me. But that's what it is all the same. That's why we're having dinner together. To make decisions. Did you know that our accountant thinks our building should be sold at the earliest possible moment, as it would be ideal for a department store or automobile showroom? Our furnaces are old and inefficient. Same with the pressroom. The price fetched would be substantial. The newspaper would be far better off in a leafy suburb somewhere, close to the circulation base, a tax advantage, a no-brainer according to our accountant. Ned spoke up at once, adamant in opposition. The present building was only a short ride to Capitol Hill and the Pentagon and within walking distance of the Treasury and the White House. Milo, perhaps teasing a little, though teasing was not his long suit, said that perhaps distance would be an advantage. Gain perspective. A building in the suburbs would put them amid suburban life. The life of the readers instead of the lives of the sources of news. Maybe our customers deserve some consideration. Milo offered a gray smile, perhaps insincere. Ned Ayres thought his attention was elsewhere. Milo was looking for the waitress.

The silence at the table continued to gather, Milo waiting patiently for Ned's ante, if he had one. Ned took a swallow of the Rioja. Speculation was useless with Milo Passarel, whose mind took unexpected turns before it came to a full stop. Somehow Ned was reminded of the publisher's office, the long desk with the company's spreadsheets neatly stacked. The framed photographs of his family on the wall, an Emil Nolde landscape above the credenza, the deal table with its cargo of arcane journals, *Dædalus*, *Scientific American*, *Le Monde Diplomatique*, the *Sewanee Review*, the *Listener* and the *Economist*, *El País*. The journals were there for intellectual relief from the spreadsheets that would occupy him in the afternoon hours, circulation down slightly and gathering speed, want ads—classifieds, in the jargon—falling off a cliff. Each year the average age of the paper's readers advanced. The most loyal subscribers were middle-aged and older who found comfort in the crackle of newsprint. Younger readers were bewitched by the Internet, altogether more convenient and lively, a refuge the publisher, in a rare display of humor, likened to an Irish bar, loud-mouths filled up with whiskey and half-baked opinions, sarcasm the coin of the realm. A deluge of cant, the publisher said, a fact-free zone supervised by bullies, showoffs, and nutcases. They are ascendant. And they will drive us out of business.

The publisher glowered in the direction of the kitchen, eager to taste the shad roe. Ned Ayres had never heard him employ slang, certainly nothing demeaning about the Irish—his own tribe, although he was not observant. Milo Passarel seemed to transcend the normal alliances, race, nationality, religion. Once he described himself as a freethinker but did not explain what that meant precisely and how it applied to his own life, if it applied at all. Now the publisher took another sip of wine.

The paper's revenues are down this quarter, he said. And expenses are rising, in part because of our own efforts to gain a seat at the Internet table, unsuccessful so far. People like it all right but they don't want to pay for it. They want it free, and when they don't get it free they're annoyed and think we can't be trusted. Milo went on about the price of newsprint, up and up again. Pension contributions are up, though there's some fudging. He said, It's only a matter of time before the news budget has to be looked at in a serious way.

That's why we're here, Ned.

I think I get the picture, Ned said. Thing is, with the paper going digital, think of the savings: all those trucks and their drivers, too, and the pressroom and the accounting that goes into subscriptions. You're saving a fortune.

The foreign file is costing a fortune.

Our jewel in the crown, Ned said.

An ornament, I agree, the publisher said. But nevertheless I want you to look at the news budget and see what you can do right away. Here's the point: not one single trend line is positive, not one. And where is our dinner, for godsakes.

Just then the waitress was at the table, murmuring apologies. Ned noticed her accent and asked where she was from. Greece, she said, and smiled. When she moved her head a comma of auburn hair fell over her left eye. She was enchanting, alluring in her white blouse and black miniskirt. She smiled tentatively and went away. Milo Passarel looked fondly at the plates of shad roe, a rasher of bacon on the side. Nicest thing about spring, the publisher said. Spring brings shad roe. Our local delicacy. Thank God for reliable tides.

But we were talking about the newsroom, Milo said. Look everywhere, look high and low. And when you begin to cut, cut like this—and he drove his dinner knife through the largest lobe and began to eat.

Ned was silent, thinking that publishers always took a dark view of things. Ned's task was to determine just how far Milo Passarel was prepared to go. He said, You mean real cuts. Cuts that go bone-deep. I can stuff Latin America right now, Ned went on. Hire a stringer instead. The man we have is excellent, as you know. Energetic. First-rate mind. Keeps expenses down. He might stay on as a stringer if we made it attractive. Or, Ned said, more drastic. Close down Madrid.

Milo said, Leave Madrid alone.

But I have to look at all the possibilities.

Madrid is not one of them.

Okay, Milo.

There's going to be more of this, the publisher said. In the newsroom and elsewhere. It's necessary.

And unfortunate, Ned said. The paper's journalism has never been better. And never been less read.

That's one way of looking at it, the publisher said. His voice was grudging.

Ned smiled. Do we have to destroy the paper in order to save it? And the moment he made the remark he regretted it, a slippery remark, a show-the-flag remark meant as an assertion of editorial independence, but now it sounded churlish.

Milo Passarel did not smile back. He said instead, Are you on board?

Of course, Ned said.

I can't do it alone, Milo said. And even if I could, I wouldn't want to. I have no interest in going it alone. We have to fly into this together. This job is *primero*. I have to know if I can count on you.

You always have, Ned said.

This is a new phase, Ned. I mean to clean up the balance sheet.

A second helping of shad roe arrived. The waitress asked if they liked their meal, and Ned said they did. And what's your name? Gretta, she said. Her voice was soft, and when the comma of hair fell once more, she pushed it back and slid away. They ate in silence. The room was quiet except for the rustle of newsprint from those dining alone. Milo looked up and called for Gretta to bring them another bottle of wine. Ned peered over the rim of his glass at Milo's frown, from which all courtesy had vanished, his eyes half shut, his cheeks red. "Clean up the balance sheet" had a particular meaning in the newspaper business, as in other businesses, including, Ned supposed, the used car business, where it meant, Clean the car before you sell it. Set the odometer back a believable twenty thousand miles, give it that new-car smell. For the moment Ned was nonplussed, and then the wine arrived, Gretta pouring slowly. Milo was busy cutting the shad roe, not very expertly. Gretta vanished. Ned thought the fish too salty and its appearance too reminiscent of human brain matter. The bacon was good, though. Ned watched Gretta stopping by the other tables.

She was beautifully built and slow-moving, taking her time with each table. She moved with élan, always smiling, actually more grin than smile, a grin being less neutral. He wondered what she was doing in this fussy men's club. She could be a model or an actress. She seemed self-possessed in the best way, meaning without presumption. Good at her job. She was built for Matisse, especially the grin.

Milo said, Will you stop looking at that girl, please?

Hard not to, Ned said.

Too young, Ned.

I was thinking. Maybe she's a girl with a grandfather complex.

Milo laughed at that, his mood apparently improving.

Milo Passarel was large of build, well over six feet in height with thinning gray hair and restless hands. His firm jaw and deeply lined face recalled one of Leonardo da Vinci's pencil-drawn anatomy lessons. Milo had the look just then of an Italian grandee, one who could take care of himself should the occasion arise. He was, on most occasions, even-tempered, affable when the situation called for it. Ned had been his editor in chief for three decades. They were not friends in that they knew very little about each other's personal life. They were colleagues and in a certain sense collaborators. Ned Ayres was the public face of the newspaper. Milo Passarel was content to remain in the background, in fact insisted on it. He was uncomfortable in crowds. He did not want to be recognized on the street nor asked to give speeches. He never gave a speech. Now and then one of the glossy magazines would attempt a profile, but the attempt always fell short because Milo Passarel retreated behind his kindly smile and deferred to Ned Ayres, always in the room to add a detail or subtract one. Faced with a probing question, Ned would laugh and say, Oh, no. We don't go there and you shouldn't either. The interviews became a vicious little game of Go Fish until the publisher tired of it, looked at his watch, and called it quits. Milo's office was immaculate, the spreadsheets now tucked away, invisible and unmentioned. In fact, Milo's insistence on anonymity and the most severe privacy was not unusual for a newspaper publisher, many of whom believed that the normal rules did not apply to them. With Milo, anonymity seemed to be a condition of employment. Occasionally, out somewhere or at a meeting, Ned observed Milo Passarel glance into a mirror with a sly look, as if to say, Fooled you again. But who was "you"? Whom, exactly, was he fooling? Ned had concluded that his publisher believed he was fooling everyone and anyone. In a moment of conceit he might have thought he was contributing to a legend, a man as reclusive as Howard Hughes. Perhaps what annoyed him was publicity itself, any sort of notoriety. Naturally there were suspicions that Milo Passarel had a secret life, a worldly life that could not stand scrutiny. A life that would not play well in daylight's glare or on the front page of a tabloid newspaper. These suspicions were false. He did look upon his job as a civilian version of trench warfare that made him vigilant. His private life was exemplary, most ordinary, law-abiding, strait-laced. It's fair to add that, like pharaohs and kings, like all the explorers of the ancient world, when Milo Passarel arrived home in the evening the first thing he did was take a bath. In the warmth of his tub he thought often of his father, who had presided over a world of plenty. The newspaper had been a cash register, no expense spared. Milo wiggled his toes and recalled that when a correspondent went to Indochina, he traveled PanAm, first class, the envy of his peers.

Milo Passarel had a wife who was seldom seen and two married daughters who lived in Europe. Milo and his wife flew to Spain every few months for long weekends with "the girls," their artist husbands, and the grandchildren. He confessed once to Ned Ayres that he felt more at home in Spain than he did in America; and then he fell silent, realizing he had given up an incriminating fact. When young he had taken a graduate course at the university in Salamanca but dutifully left the university when his father suffered the first of two heart attacks. He was needed at the paper, no excuses. Milo Sr. would be lucky to live another year or so— which, in the event, turned out to be twenty-one years. So Milo Jr. was installed as associate publisher, sent to Harvard Business School for a year, and returned with a knowledge of spreadsheets. Milo had always been good with numbers, having received a degree in applied mathematics. He, his wife, and the girls settled in a four-story row house on 34th Street in Georgetown. His office at the paper was next to his father's, the better to see how a real publisher operated. Throwing his weight around, as Milo Jr. put it to his wife, Lana. They led a sedate, uncomplicated life, very much a family. When they went on vacation, the girls always went with them. The month of August was spent in Spain, first the Costa Blanca south of Barcelona, and when that filled up with Germans they went to San Sabastian. They made one more stop and settled finally in Granada, a pretty whitewashed villa north of the city, the bulk of the Alhambra in clear sight from their patio.

They came to love Spanish food and the Spanish temperament and the relaxed way of life, a nap in the afternoon and dinner at ten p.m. They liked the rough laughter in the streets and tabernas. The Spanish people were composed and dignified. Behind their composure they were a passionate people with austere souls, not a contradiction when Milo thought about it. The family's guide through the Spanish labyrinth was the paper's Madrid bureau chief, Susan Griffin, a bon vivant who had lived in Madrid for forty years. She knew everyone in the city, including the king and queen. She knew the matador El Cordobés, and her husband, Harold, knew everyone else, police officials and the foreign minister, flamenco dancers and the chef at the Ritz. Harold wrote mystery novels, one a year. Susan and Harold Griffin were the Passarels' guide to Spain high and low. For the long weekends and the month of August Milo could forget about the paper. Ned Ayres was instructed not to bother the publisher except for an emergency of the most serious character. Nor to expect too much copy from Susan Griffin, who brought such merriment into the family's life.

Each August Milo and Ms. Seldom Seen traveled to their villa near Granada to spend the month with their daughters, Susan and Harold often in residence. Milo had bought a van seating ten people for journeys into the backcountry to search for birds. They were a family of birders, the Griffins too. When not birding, Milo and Lana took long lunches and even longer naps, rising at six to mix mild cocktails and dine amid their backyard cedar trees, where they discussed the churches of the region and the grottoes of the hillsides. They were often joined by the Griffins, who brought the latest Madrid gossip, usually hilarious and subterranean in the Spanish manner. The film community, such as it was, made a commedia dell'arte all its own. Susan Griffin confessed that when she first met Milo and Lana, she thought them dour and uncommunicative; perhaps the word was unresponsive. But they improved with age and now she saw them in a different light altogether. Milo spoke only a little Spanish, but his accent was superb and in his espadrilles and his straw hat he easily passed as a native, or if not native, then Portuguese. His height and his bearing lent him authority. Señor Milo, the villagers called him, an important American publisher who tipped generously and remembered everyone's name and never asked awkward questions. He himself volunteered little, perhaps a comment on the weather or on an unusual bird sighting.

All this information came from Susan Griffin, who retailed it to Ned Ayres on her biennial visits to Washington.

Some people are temperamentally displaced, Susan said. They are in one place and imagine themselves in another. There are two Milos that I know of. Maybe there's a third somewhere, known only to Lana or the children. But you should see them in Spain at the end of the evening, laughing uproariously, slightly tipsy from the flasks of Rioja. The party never broke up before midnight and sometimes went on much later.

You would not recognize him, Ned.

Of course the paper and its affairs were never mentioned.

That was the Rule.

The Passarel Rule, Lana called it.

Violate the Rule and you're not asked back.

Susan said, He's a charming man, Ned. Witty, beautiful manners, quiet disposition. That Leonardo head brown from the sun even though he always wore a hat. Go figure. And Lana was good company once you got her going, which was not hard to do. I always tried to see them off at the end of the month, not that he showed any appreciation. You see, he was already in Washington mode, a dark suit and a fedora, a leather briefcase, a copy of the *Financial Times* in his jacket pocket. He was going home to Washington but that was not where he wanted to be, so he removed his sunglasses and pulled on his American personality. I was often impertinent with him but he never seemed to mind. When I asked him what he thought when he thought about Washington, and he said, Spreadsheets, I had to ask him what they were because we do not have spreadsheets in Spain. So he explained about the spreadsheets and their contribution to an understanding of the bottom line, a mudslide of declining revenues. He was talking about the government but he meant the newspaper, his voice rising as he went along. I never heard him utter one word about the paper's troubles, and that was frustrating to me, Susan said, because I had heard all the rumors and was eager to know how many of them were true as opposed to the usual sloppy gossip. In some respects he reminded me of an art collector looking at his Old Masters and realizing he was on the downside of things, as if his beauties were—quaint. I think that was how he thought about his paper. Whenever we got near the subject, even when someone mentioned a piece in the *Herald Tribune* or the *FT*, Lana put a finger to her lips and shook her head. Off limits. *Verboten. Interdit.* Not to be discussed in Milo's hearing. I think that was Lana's job, keeping the business caged so that Milo could run free, at least for those days when he was in Spain. My Harold was baffled by him, and her, too. People in the newspaper business loved it. You could say they loved it to death. Couldn't live without it, and here was the publisher of one of the most important papers in America who preferred a backwater region in a backwater country to spend his summers. He could be dining at Chequers or shooting pheasant in the Sologne, yet here he was in the Spanish countryside, the *campo*. It was a *campo* all right. Like any well-fixed tourist from Chicago or Houston, content in his cedar grove, looking at churches and stalking birds, reading *Dædalus* in his spare time, a Cinzano and soda at the end of the afternoon. Well, Susan said, my Harold was always a bit of a romantic about the newspaper business. I think, secretly, Harold wanted to own one. But he didn't have the money, so he turned to mystery novels instead.

Fact is, Susan said, Milo's a puzzle. Probably a good idea not to probe too deeply. Milo wouldn't like it. He'd clam up. When you're talking to Milo you're pretty much talking on his terms.

He took his privacy seriously, did Milo. Susan Griffin thought a moment and added, Probably the better word is anonymity. But, that aside, he and Lana were wonderful to be with. But I would never have cast Milo as a newspaper proprietor, never in a million years. Odd thing is, he's inquisitive. Lana, too. Spanish indifference was especially appealing to a certain kind of American, the American who wanted nothing more than to be left alone. He liked it that the Spanish had no discernible foreign policy. They had let Gibraltar go its own way. Gibraltar and its adorable apes. They just—let it go.

The Passarel villa was nicely situated in the foothills of the high sierra above the Alhambra. In the late afternoon Milo watched the westering sun and the fantastic shadows cast on the Alhambra, the all-but-last stand of the Moors at Granada. Milo believed that Spain would be forever divided owing to the defeat of the Moors on the Iberian Peninsula and that Spain would be forever alienated from Europe owing to the Muslim question. Spain was mired in the Middle Ages without knowing it. Despite the many foreigners among them, the Spanish looked inward, tight-lipped.

Milo Passarel and his family had spent twenty years in the villa on the slopes above the Alhambra and never had a conversation with Spanish friends about their civil war. The war was a chasm in their memory, visible, all but tangible, but never discussed. Milo had a theory that the Spanish were horrified at what they had done to one another, savagery beyond comprehension, both sides, a war that arrived from deep in their hearts, in some respects a reenactment of the Inquisition that flourished in the fifteenth century but had its roots in a much earlier time. A question of heretics. The Inquisition was everywhere in Europe, but the Spanish had a special taste for death by burning, books part of the bonfire. Heretical books. Blasphemous books. That was another of Milo's gloomy observations. Not widely shared, it had to be said. So Franco won his war and a great sullen silence was the result. To his countrymen, the generalissimo said in effect, I will give you peace, and the price you will pay is silence. He meant obedience, and so the Spanish fell into a kind of time warp, the chasm. But the warp had its beneficial aspects. It saved them from the carnage of the Second World War, Spain remaining neutral and leaning in the direction of Berlin, but never too far in that direction, Franco being smarter than he looked or sounded. The nation was frightened and exhausted after its own struggle. This was no small gift. Having avoided the First World War as well, Spain remained on the margins of European history, singular and ignored except for the hordes of tourists when the weather turned cold in the north. It was also true that for many years the ground yielded corpses, some buried en masse; merchants in one space, laboring men in another. Also women of both castes. In that way the legacy of the Spanish war was never-ending. The silence that Franco sought was the silence of the grave. In time, naturally, the younger generation came of age. Hard to know what to make of that generation. They did love *futbol*.

Milo was fascinated by all this, Susan said that night in Washington. Milo believed that everything of significance in Spain happened out of sight. At some level, perhaps the Spanish people did not want to know. They were content not knowing. Knowing, a citizen became an accomplice, and Franco more or less forbade that. He was dead but his spirit was in the fabric of life, the way Hitler and Stalin were part of the fabric of Germany and the Soviet Union. But this, too: they were an attractive people, a people with depth, reticent, dark-souled, people for the most part without envy. A people who understood the value of silence. Circumspection.

What I never understood, Susan said, was Milo's attraction to the Spanish condition. He was in thrall to it as if he owned a piece of it. Or was entitled to a piece of it. So it was interesting—no, weird—listening to Milo when he would have the neighbors to dinner along with Harold and me. There was Don Carlos and Don Fernando and their quiet wives, and Milo would keep edging closer to the Spanish labyrinth. He would deliver a few thoughtful remarks about the American press and then urge his guests to say a word about their own newspapers, the Madrid press and the others. His guests looked up, baffled. Don Carlos said he never read the papers, trusting instead to friends, some of whom were in the government or industries close to the government. Don Carlos gave the impression that excellent things were happening. They were not public for the moment, but they were there, and all the Spanish people required was some patience—

And Milo pounced, Susan said. Which you have in abundance, Milo said with a smile.

Yes, we are a patient people.

The opposite of Americans, Milo said, who are impatient, volatile, frequently corrupt. All this said with a smile, whereupon Don Carlos changed the subject, sensing turbulence ahead.

Susan said, One night Milo had too much to drink, rare for him. He began to talk about the Alhambra and the spell it cast. Its great rooms and towering ceilings, Muslim decoration—not a human face or form to be found on its walls. Its vast silence, its mystery, its many secrets, its ghosts from a medieval past. He went on and on as we all sat and listened. For the life of me, Susan said, I cannot figure how he reconciled his two domains, Andalusia and

Washington. For certain he had concocted a mythical Spain, the Spain of centuries past. The time Spain ruled the known world. But he was not entirely wrong about the Spanish situation today. Thank God for the king, despite his lapses.

He thought about privacy, too, Susan Griffen went on. How much of it you were owed, or if you were owed anything. And how much governments were owed. I ventured the thought that one could be suffocated by secrets and the ghosts that held them. No, Milo said. Definitely not. Secrets were a necessity, for people and governments both. When everything is known, nothing is safe.

Did he say that? Ned Ayres asked. Really?

Really. He was quite convinced.

This business about being owed —

But Susan only laughed. She said, Of course he was seduced by Goya, who he thought had a great heart. His solution to the seduction was to buy six prints of the master's Disasters of War series and hang them in the living room of his villa overlooking the Alhambra.

Milo Passarel and his wife were especially close, rarely out of each other's sight, a nation of two. They were both great readers, always a book in their hands. Lana always came to Spain with a project, one summer reading Proust, the next learning German. I think I am not telling a tale, Susan Griffin said, but I never saw her read a newspaper, even her husband's paper, which was pouched daily from Washington. She is not quite of this world, Lana Passarel. Perhaps neither of them is. But they are wonderful to be around so long as you appreciate the rhythms of the nineteenth century. Milo had projects of his own, gardening, rereading Homer. They were highly concentrated, both of them, but good to be around. All this time I wondered how Milo managed the chore of publishing a newspaper. Still, I always looked forward to their visits, Susan said, as I believe they looked forward to mine. They certainly didn't treat me as an employee, more an expatriate relative.

So you know, Susan said, I heard him once describe the paper's content as "clutter." So much of it that the reader could not concentrate. Milo sought focus. He thought the reader should seek focus. He had the idea that the paper was, at its essence, chaotic. The train wreck and the tax bill side by side on page one. I objected, in a mild sort of way. I wasn't sure if he was joking or not joking.

Not joking, Ned said.

In some strange sense he wanted to follow the physician's creed. Do no harm. Can you imagine?

Ned smiled. It's so—off the point.

I asked him once about his father, Susan said. What kind of man he was.

Milo said, Not a quality man.

I was taken aback but I did press on. I laughed and asked what he meant. What qualities exactly?

Milo waited a moment before answering. I think he wanted to change the subject but a reply was irresistible. My father was a pseudo-politician, Milo said at last. All politics. Morning, noon, and night, politics. The old man was in politics up to his ears, couldn't get enough of politics. Congressional politics, ideological politics. Kingmaking, he called it. He lived for election years, which states were in play and which weren't. Where the smart money was and where it was going. He commissioned polls and ran them in the newspaper. Father was always looking for a candidate who fit the times, an attitude that allowed him to define the times and the man, both. He was a tiresome man, a one-note father. He liked to entertain his political friends in the company dining room, plenty to eat and drink. Lunches could last until four, five in the afternoon. He claimed to have elected three presidents by fair means and foul. Father set a high bar, or thought he did. Also, he was a gambler, cards mostly. I don't know, Milo said, precisely what that added to his personality, but it added something.

I couldn't think of what to reply, Susan said, so I said, I'm sorry. Inane, no? But that was what came to mind.

Ned's memory stirred. He had lost the thread. He said, Tell me more about the "Do no harm." Did he explain how you went about that?

That was my idea, Susan said. My inference, I should say.

I wonder how that goal could be achieved.

Through caution, Susan said, and laughed.

A cautious newspaper, Ned said.

I suppose a newspaper with a conscience, Susan said. A newspaper that did not throw its weight around.

They were having a drink in Ned's apartment near Dupont Circle, and when silence fell neither of them seemed to mind. The silence was companionable. Dusk gathered and Ned moved to switch on the standing lamps, but darkness prevailed. Susan said something about liking his apartment, so open and close to the office, a quiet place. Susan stole a look at her watch. She was due at the Passarels' in thirty minutes and returning to Spain in the morning. Harold had the flu. The weather in Madrid was wretched, an inversion that dirtied the air. Susan was eager to go home, but she hated the inversions. Ned Ayres was lost in thought, but at last he said, Probably the word we're seeking is modesty. Not helpful, is it? Not applicable. Not the solution. Maybe not even the question. Susan Griffin finished her glass and looked up. Ned's face was in shadow. She wondered why he had never married. Well, he was married to the newspaper. That was clear enough. She glanced once again at her wristwatch and stood, stretching. In a voice scarcely louder than a whisper, she said that there could be a lesson in music, the composition of it, harmony, melody, and rhythm. In Western music the first two are dominant, with rhythm a kind of decoration. In Indian music melody and rhythm control the piece, with harmony irrelevant or an afterthought. Philip Glass's observation, and it sounds right to me. Apply this to a newspaper and harmony is absent also. In fact harmony would be seen as slant. A romantic virtue. That's why to the untrained ear Indian music is difficult. It's a closed door. Could it be that what is sought in a newspaper is harmony? What do you think?

Ned Ayres had no idea what to think. He said unconvincingly, Huh.

Indian music is unfulfilled. Painful for the most part unless you are of the cognoscenti, like Glass.

Well, she said. Never mind.

Ned said, You're on to something. I don't know what.

By the way, Susan said, Milo called his father a shrimp.

Ned was now in another place altogether and did not reply.

Definitely a shrimp with a Napoleonic complex.

In spades, Ned said.

In a tricorn hat, said Susan.

I'll tell you this, she went on. She had collected her coat and her hand was on the doorknob. We were sitting on the porch of Milo's villa. The temperature was in the nineties, everyone slick with sweat. Mosquitoes abounded. The Alhambra below us simmered in the heat, waves of it rising. The Alhambra had the aspect of a mirage. Tourists were crawling all over the building, the people tiny as ants. Milo was staring at the Alhambra, deep in thought. He abruptly turned his head to look at the summit of the sierra. He said something about how the snow was white as milk. I had one last question.

And his father, your grandfather. What was he like?

He liked music, Milo said.

From the hammock, Lana said in her quiet way, *Basta* with the genealogy.

Milo smiled and held up the magazine he had been reading. I think it was *Dædalus*. And replied, Did you know that the world was running out of food?

So much gossip in our business, more than any other business, because reporters and editors are trained snoops. That's what we do, Susan said, snoop where we can and share the results, and all the better if the results are combustible. Revelatory. I suppose you could say that we set the bar. But as I'm sure you noticed, Ned, we never share the Milo results with our readers. Or our competition. That's out of bounds. It's in-house. Milo Passarel has our fate in his hands and so we protect him. Protect his wife, if it comes to that. So the playing field is a little bit uneven. His privacy is our privacy, don't you see? One of those things . . . well, we don't inquire too closely.

It was obvious that Milo Passarel was miscast as a newspaper publisher—not that his father was a model either. But the father's ambitions were normal for the times. He published the paper to have an influence on things, the occupant of the White House, the provisions of the new tax bill, the vacancy on the Supreme Court. In any case, if there was a top table in sight, Milo's father intended to be seated at it. Milo was far from that. Milo had no feel for the meaning of newspaper publishing. Milo was an artist with no instinct for perspective. A myopic artist with no grasp of where one thing fit into another thing and sooner or later you had a policy. He was unable to lose himself in it. He truly didn't like the business. It was a chore for him, a duty dance. But his inheritance was a fact of life, like the dimple on his chin. Nothing to be done about it. Milo did have an almost mystical faith in his Harvard spreadsheets, but that was all he had, no seat-of-the-pants understanding of the nature of the business and its importance to the civic life of the nation. A newspaper, after all, is presenting its version of a song, that day's melody. What the world looked like that day and what it might look like tomorrow so that the reader had some idea where he fit in. The paper was a species of seismology, where things were safe and where they weren't safe, never omitting the trivial: the National League standings or the saga of the senator and the page boy. Of course all that could be gathered at the touch of a fingernail on a cell phone. Perhaps not the seismology. Seismology required a paragraph or better.

Susan Griffin thought that when Milo looked at the Alhambra, its graceful lines, its great age and specific mystique, he saw his newspaper at the threshold of a long and certain decline, an artifact for anyone interested in past time, its manners, its morals, its aspirations and discipline, its deceits and its triumphs. Legends. Milo Passarel was a man who noticed things, and what he noticed from the porch of his villa were the crowds, so many of them Asian—who took pictures of themselves. They were not bewitched. They did not even seem interested. Well, it was only a building. One needed nothing special to enjoy it or draw a lesson from it. No need to know the code, the password, the special key, or the secret handshake. It did help to know the history. Milo did think that in certain respects the Alhambra mirrored the newspaper business. Yet he was not the ideal witness. Milo listened to the faint rhythms of the guitars and scrutinized the inner and outer Alhambra and did not believe one inch of it.

It was sublime once, he said. Now it's a picture gallery.

Susan Griffin said, You can't believe that.

But I do. It's in decline and has been for centuries. It is now a place where Asian peoples come to take pictures of themselves. Americans and European peoples, too, as if the Alhambra were a great mirror. In fact it is the very epitome of decline. Not a tomb, not a place of worship, not even a simple memorial. But even so, Milo conceded, it is durable and handsome in its own fashion. The Alhambra has lasted a very long time. Wouldn't you say there's something stealthy about it? Perhaps it will last another eleven centuries, a conundrum to ponder. The astrologers believe that to be the case and they are not always wrong.

There are very many surprising things in the world, Milo said, and the humanist's great task is to stay surprised, even with what is forbidden.

Over the years, decades now, Lana Passarel and Susan Griffin became great friends. Lana's natural reserve fell away in the Spanish heat. They lunched often together, either in Madrid or in Granada, sitting outside under an awning or an umbrella. Milo and Harold would be off somewhere, lunching with one or another of Harold's sources, a Treasury official or one of the curators at the Prado. Lana was curious about Susan's professional life, the stories she liked and the ones she didn't. She made frequent trips to Morocco and Tunisia, her "patches," as she called them. Susan always had a fresh anecdote concerning the beastly way the North Africans treated women—though, on the whole, better than the Arabs farther to the east. Lana had a few Washington stories, not very interesting, at least to her. Susan ate them up. Washington had always been a mystery to her, and the longer she stayed away from the United States the more mysterious it became. Halfway through lunch they began to talk about their husbands, the state of their health, their moodiness and irritability. Lana confided that Milo had had some heart trouble and was on a diet. He had lost weight, particularly around the middle, and none of his trousers fit properly. Susan gave Lana the name of Harold's tailor in Madrid. And Harold, too, was troubled by lazy bowel syndrome. He had medication for it but the medication wasn't working. Isn't it terrible to see them grow old? And then, their voices lowered, they would speak of their own complaints, a breast cancer scare for Lana, spells of depression for Susan. She had pills for it but they worked only marginally. Pills are useless for something so deep down; it's like having three thumbs or one eye out of whack. Oh, my dear, Lana said, we're getting old! Susan refused to hear of it, aging and illness, and proposed a visit to the bullfights, some entertainment *a las cinco de la tarde*.

Oh, golly, Lana said. Do we have to?

Susan was an aficionada, liking the spectacle, the dance and the dancer. She did not care for the blood that was involved but understood that blood was part of the spectacle, as much ritual as spectacle, not exactly a discordant note but definitely Wagnerian. Lana was repulsed at first but came around as she listened to Susan describe the formality of the ritual, a three-act opera in most cases. Susan did hope that they never saw a corrida with the matador gored, the horn nearly always entering the groin or close to the groin, a ghastly finish to a rough ballet that was quite beautiful once you understood the scenario. Of course it was brutal. The Spanish were brutal, not always but often enough. Milo and Harold had no interest in corrida, a barbarian entertainment, so they stayed behind and welcomed their wives for a meal after the event, inquiring into the body count and the bull's fate and the wild cheering that accompanied it all. If in Madrid, they dined at the Ritz, if in Granada, at the Alhambra Palace Hotel, the meal always late in the evening. Harold often brought someone with him, an official at the Royal Palace or someone from the army or the Guardia Civil. Milo liked to hear stories of palace life and the underworld, stories that never found their way into the newspaper. Lana and Susan sat together so they could reprise the corrida, the matador as silky as an eel, the coup de grâce immaculate and brief.

That evening at the Ritz in Madrid was the last time they dined together. Lana was unusually talkative, describing what she and Susan saw in the arena. By then Lana had learned the lingo, the picadors, the veronica pivot, the puntillo the matador was forced to use in the event the bull refused to die by the sword, an embarrassment all around. Halfway through the first course the policeman left the table to take a telephone call and did not return. He sent one of the waiters to explain: there was an emergency in the Retiro. As the meal wore on, their table became hilarious generally, Harold telling stories nonstop. One bottle of Rioja after another. Milo was enthralled. He said he felt twenty years younger. Lana was as spirited as a schoolgirl experiencing the wider world for the first time. The cries of the spectators, the president of the arena applauding. That night at the Ritz was a revelation, not because it was new but because it was so intimate. As they were drinking coffee after dinner, Lana turned to Milo and said, We have found Xanadu. This is our place. I'd like to stay one more month, two months. Could we do that? And if not, why not? Isn't it fun? Aren't we having the best time? Her eyes were shining. Milo thought she had never looked happier. Lana had been troubled lately but now her trouble had vanished in a storm of amiability and trust. She said, We are so far from the instability of America.

That night, Harold died in his sleep. Susan called, her voice barely under control. She was hysterical, and so Milo and Lana threw on their clothes and drove at once to the Griffin apartment near the Plaza de España. An ambulance was parked on the sidewalk. Milo explained that they were friends of Señor and Señora Griffin and were admitted at once. Susan was lying down and Lana went to her and took her up in a long embrace. Milo spoke to the doctor, who was sitting at Harold's desk writing his report. A thunderous heart attack, the doctor said. He died almost at once. You must take care of his wife. She is heartsick. She must not be left alone.

Milo said he understood and asked if he could pay whatever charges there were.

There are no charges, the doctor said, sounding aggrieved.

I am happy to do so, Milo said.

We will leave now, the doctor said. There is no more to be done.

They were our closest friends, Milo said.

You must look after Señora Griffin.

Yes, we shall.

She needs a doctor's care. This was evidently a shock. I believe she was not aware of any heart trouble.

She was not, Milo said.

I hope she recovers. I have seen cases like this one.

Difficult, Milo said.

Yes, very difficult.

If you had arrived earlier, Milo began.

The doctor continued to write. He was young, with an El Greco face and black hair. Not yet thirty, Milo guessed, an aloof doctor who did not look up from the notebook when he replied, It would have made no difference, none whatever. You must accept that as the truth.

Then Lana was at his side. You go along, she said. I will stay here with Susan. She must not be alone tonight.

You're sure? Milo asked.

Go along, Lana said.

All right, he said. What about you?

I'll be fine, don't worry.

Milo nodded. The room seemed to him dangerous, as if inhabited by malevolent spirits whose work was not yet completed. He opened a window to let the night air in. The street below was silent in these early hours of the morning.

The doctor said good night to them both and departed. Then the stretcher-bearers were in the room with Harold Griffin's remains wrapped in a white winding-sheet. Milo held the door as they, too, departed. Then the room was silent, but uneasy, too. Lana went into Susan's bedroom and closed the door. Milo stood for a long moment with his hands on the windowsill, listening to the muffled sounds from the bedroom. He watched the stretcher-bearers load Harold Griffin into the ambulance and in a minute they were gone, without sirens and only the red light slowly turning. That was it, he thought. The world turned and in an instant of time was unfamiliar. The apartment was unfamiliar, though he had been in it many, many times over the years. He turned from the window and went to the kitchen for a glass of water. He decided not to go to the hotel. He would remain here in the event he was needed. Offer advice, write a check, stand guard. He stepped to the telephone, thinking he should call Ayres. There was an obituary to be written. But in the end he did nothing. The obituary could wait.

Harold Griffin was virtually unknown in America. His books were written in Spanish, published in Spain.

At the table in Milo Passarel's Washington club the silence lengthened. The waitress Gretta glided by to place the check on the table for Milo's signature. Milo looked up and said, Bring us two glasses of port, if you please. Gretta grinned fractionally and slipped away. Milo and Ned Ayres were alone in the dining room, Ned wondering what he could add in the way of a confidence-builder. The conversation had led nowhere. Milo was distracted, apparently back in Spain as he so often was. Milo had thought through the newspaper situation and had decided that the game was up. What Milo saw was the Irish bar and he thought, What was the point? It seemed to him that the struggle was already lost and without lament, except for people in the business. Was this competition worth his while? If you owned a Van Gogh, why on earth would you exchange it for a Koons? At these moments Milo often thought of Andalusia and its comforts, the villa in the high sierra, his books and his music, a mild cocktail at the end of the day, his grandchildren at his feet, Susan Griffin with her lurid tales of Madrid and its dependencies. She and Lana spoke on the telephone every day and the most Susan could say was that the fog was beginning to lift, slowly, with hesitation; she found it difficult to speak Harold's name, and that was why she wished the Passarels would return to Granada . . . Milo felt the same way about the newspaper. The short-term solution was to cut the budget, cut the size of the newspaper, cut staff. There was no long-term solution. So perhaps he was a visionary after all. Perhaps he had second sight. His view of the future was one of ruin, not today or tomorrow but soon and forever. These thoughts preoccupied him, his only true confidante his wife. Ned Ayres was less helpful.

Ned said at last, I know you're troubled by all this. Anyone would be. I am. But the paper is essential. It's essential to the life of this city, federal business. It's a gut check for us, Ned went on, and looked at Milo to see if he understood the expression, and apparently he did because he nodded in agreement. The paper is fundamentally sound, Ned said, and Milo smiled because that was Hoover's phrase to describe the American economy during the Great Depression. Our bottom lines are still relatively strong, Ned went on. We can't walk away or sell it to some thug on Wall Street. It's—cowardly.

Milo looked up, expressionless but for his thin smile.

I'll find the ways and means to make the cuts you want.

The paper's a wasting asset, Milo said.

I won't touch Madrid. That's a promise.

It's still a wasting asset, Milo said.

No sir, Ned said in a kind of growl. It's a beautiful paper. It's an essential paper in this city. Ned cleared his throat and went on to describe articles published in the past few months, groundbreaking work, admired in the trade. *We set the agenda*, he said, and began to speak of Washington in the most intimate terms, as if he were describing the smallest town in the world—Herman, Indiana, with monuments.

Milo Passarel listened without any change of expression, unless his small sigh was an expression. He did not reply. Sitting lost in thought, sipping espresso, he watched Gretta approach with two glasses of tawny port on a little silver salver. In the half light of the dining room her face was in shadow but no less alluring. She said, Are you enjoying yourselves, gentlemen? We are, Ned said. Tell me something, Gretta. Do you read the newspapers? Oh, no, she said. I am a classicist. I read the ancient Greeks, Homer and the playwrights. That grin again, and a bold stare to go with it. She added, But I have to say to you that the dining room is closed. Milo said, We will not be long. We are almost finished here. Thank you, Gretta said, and glided away once more.

They sipped their port. Ned was uncertain whether Milo was fully awake. Lately he had a way of nodding off, not asleep but not fully conscious either. He was comfortable in some intermediate zone. Milo said, Lana and I had a particularly good time in Spain last summer, until the last week, when Harold passed. It was dreadful. Poor Susan almost lost her mind. It was so unexpected, and she and Harold were so close they could read each other's minds, but not this time. It brings you up short, something like that. Death concentrates your mind, and not in a particularly helpful way. Did I tell you we had tea with the king and his son? Susan Griffin set it up, so she was there, too, and a good thing because she knew the questions to ask. I mean, she knew what was on his mind. Nothing special about it, but there aren't very many of them around anymore, kings. He seemed to enjoy being king. He's quite tall, you know. I have the idea that kings should be tall. Being tall becomes them. Franco was short. He had a peasant's face and build and manner and yet was revered by his troops. On the other hand, maybe they were just frightened by him, his confidence and his power, what he was capable of, which was pretty much anything. He distrusted people. He distrusted Europe. He wanted Spain to remain apart, under his thumb. So we had a nice conversation over tea and cakes but Franco did not figure in the conversation. I felt it would be impolite to ask the king about the circumstances leading to his ascension to the throne, all Franco's doing to allow for an orderly changing of the guard, so to speak. In any case, Franco was long dead and only his shadow remained, and it is a long shadow. The queen was not present during our tea. She had apparently gone horseback riding that day.

Ned smiled politely, wondering where this was going.

Milo said, For the whole month the weather was perfect, never a cloud in the sky. I spent more time than usual in the Alhambra, a marvel that depends not on architecture but on geometry. Geomancy, too. The zodiac plays a role. It's built on mathematical principles. In the ninth century artisans from all over the known world came to work on the Alhambra. The dates are in disarray. Facts unverified. That's what I like about it, Milo said. What a sight it must have been, the construction. A wonder of the world. Milo sat back and sipped his port. He said quietly, What I want is a normal life.

Ned Ayres did not know what to say to that.

It's my turn, Milo said.

Ned squinted across the table but did not reply.

Lana agrees with me.

Of course, Ned said. When did she not?

Beautiful soft Andalusian summers.

Sounds good, Milo said.

We need new blood. In my chair and your chair, too.

Are you moving me out, Milo?

The publisher did not answer. He was lost in thought, sipping port.

Andalusian summers, Ned said, and swallowed the dregs of his port. He said, Jesus, Milo. You can't give it up like that. You can't say fuck it and walk away, he added in a voice louder than he intended.

My children have no interest in the paper. Why would they? They are not attracted to lost causes.

I know, Ned said.

And if they did, I would discourage them. It's no life for them, or for me either. It's like the art world. Impressionism gives way to expressionism that gives way to abstraction, and what you have finally is a blank canvas.

But three generations of your family—

One more reason, Milo said.

Now they were on the sidewalk, looking through Lafayette Park to the White House. The park was deserted but the lights of the mansion still blazed. Probably the president was giving a poker soiree. A police cruiser idled near the iron gate with its whitewashed guardhouse. Milo had been in the Oval Office but once, summoned with another publisher to keep silent on a leaked story that was a threat to national security. Milo wanted Ned with him, but the national security adviser said no, principals only. When they arrived the president was seated at his desk, flanked left and right by the secretaries of state and defense and the CIA director, who did most of the talking in his rolling southern accent. He set the scene and identified the problem, then described the seriousness of it. After the opening hellos, Milo and the other publisher did not speak for thirty minutes. A few of the details they already knew, the broad outlines, the threat. In the end the publishers agreed to hold off, wait on events. They were thanked and ushered from the president's office. In the event, the crisis was a false alarm, more embarrassment than crisis. Ned had listened to Milo's account without comment, though he raised his eyebrows when the publisher said, No harm done. The president and his men were apologetic, if distant and uninformative, as if crises were dissolved by coincidence or misapprehension, an act of fate. Human agency was not involved except at the margins. Specifically, the American government was not involved unless its benign hand could be seen as involvement. Ned Ayres had visited that dead horse many times but chose now not to speak. What was done was done. But when the government and the newspapers collaborated, harm was the consequence. No exceptions. This was the point that Milo Passarel did not grasp. Milo and his beautiful soft summers. His tea with kings. He was irresponsible, there was no other word for it. Milo was an all-points-of-the-compass man, eternally seeking refuge. That was the maddening trouble with Milo. He was elusive. You couldn't get your hands around him. He lived in a make-believe world from the distant past.

The publisher's car was idling at the curb. Milo asked if Ned wanted a ride to Dupont Circle. Ned said he didn't. He preferred to walk.

Ned said, I thought you'd have more grit, push comes to shove.

Milo answered, I have sense enough to know that the curtain has fallen. Some light remains, not much. Milo hesitated, his hand on the door handle. He said, I'm worn out. You are too, for different reasons. You just won't admit it.

Ned gave a derisory laugh. He said, This is leading nowhere. I hope you find your beautiful soft summer.

They shook hands, a fierce grip from both. Milo was stronger than he looked. He asked again if Ned wanted a ride, and Ned said he thought not and walked away to dissolve into the ten o'clock darkness. Milo watched him go but his attention was elsewhere. He was thinking of the girl Gretta, her beauty and her good cheer, her inwardness, her invincible self-possession, her mild amusement at the two old parties unable to settle their dispute, whatever it was. She hovered near their table, a worried caretaker, and then she went away to her cave or castle or wherever it was she lived. She did not read the paper. She read Homer and the tragedians. She did not read the paper because there was no place for her in it. Gretta was sublime, and the paper did not do sublime. Milo wondered what would become of her. What did she imagine for herself? A life like no other, certainly. Milo would never know, and that was the beauty of it. That was life itself, secrets and mystery that went on and on without end. She would have a life and it would be her own. It would not be public property. Milo continued to stand sentry at the car's open door as Ned Ayres disappeared into the shadows of K Street. He speculated that this girl would write a great tragedy, one as great as the works of her ancient countrymen. In the meantime she had the fussy men's club to earn her way, whichever way that was. Milo doubted he would ever see her again. He wondered if she had an Achilles to keep her company. But no. Gretta would disdain violence, so fundamental to the work of the modern world. It was the modern world. Milo looked up at the dining room of his club. A shadow paused, then passed and was gone. Confusion ruled. Old man's innocent reverie.

Six

THE GOLDEN TABLE

NED'S MANOR HOUSE was located on a thick tongue of land that poked into Chesapeake Bay, not far from Casserly's Island on the Eastern Shore of Maryland, a border state with an intemperate climate, gloomy in winter and a furnace in summer, motionless days when even the air seemed exhausted. Nothing moved in the heat, including the heavy branches of the great oaks. In times past, the fifty acres—"Wilson's Fifty," as it was known locally—had been farmed in a gentlemanly way, corn mostly, good cover for the pheasant native to the region, a shooter's paradise, geese and duck along with the pheasant. The bay abounded in shellfish. Outbuildings included a stable, an apiary, and a screened-in gazebo close by the clay tennis court. The gazebo came to be called the Summer House, usually occupied at the end of the day, rain or shine, except for the winter months.

On clear mornings when the sun was low in the eastern sky, Ned liked to patrol his property, see that things were in good order. He began around seven with a thermos of black espresso under his arm, moving slowly down the dewy path in the direction of the bay. Orioles were about. Rabbits were absent, no doubt aware of the intruder in their midst. Ned took little account of them, or the birds either. He was content enough in the near silence, defined somehow by the trill of a bird or the distant purr of a waterman's two-stroke Evinrude. A gull ghosted by, followed by a flight of snowy egrets. Every few moments Ned paused and stood still, listening to the sounds advance and retreat, heat rising as the sun gathered force, shadows diminishing. The thickness and color of this terrain was still unfamiliar to him, a wild place in the world. Beside it, his manor house looked almost cosmopolitan. There were places in the Fifty he had never visited, a woodland so thick Ned could lose himself in five minutes. There was only this one narrow carriage path. The bay was invisible save for a sliver of blue water if he raised himself on tiptoe, the change of light turning the water clergyman gray. The path itself was meandering, working slowly around the trees and bramble bushes, unwelcoming until he reached the pier where the world opened up. Looking north he could see a portion of the towering Bay Bridge; to the south was the expanse of water that led to the ocean. When he had first arrived a cat was waiting for him at the doorway. Some months ago the cat disappeared. Cats were unpredictable. Obedience was not in their nature. Still, he missed the cat, an elusive companion of sorts. When he came upon the pier Ned thought of Crusoe minus the Man. Instead of the Man, he had the cat. Before the pier was his Adirondack chair, uncomfortable but familiar. Its bright red paint had softened to a dull pink. Ned settled himself in his chair and watched the puny disturbances in the water, evidence of crab life. Elegant swimmers. Delicious. He sipped espresso and thought about his book, then lit a cigarette to help things along. The tobacco smoke rose. A straight line in the breathless air.

So much had gone unwritten. He found his stories difficult to translate, meaning the route from memory to paper. He was an editor, not a writer. Something preposterous about it, editing your own memory. Everyone knew that memory was fishy. False testimony, fingers crossed. In so many of his recollections there would be no corroboration because the principals were dead. His family, all dead. What he had was his working life and the pieces of paper that supplied verification. The flimsies, he called them, mostly garbled and often embellished—as if the raw memory was itself tainted, and below the surface much like the elegant swimmers. The flash of a claw, a bony head, and a black eye. Hopeless.

Even so, on this lovely Maryland morning he was pondering the art of the interview and therefore summoned the gravelly yet grudging voice of the celebrated South American poet of volcanic temperament whose American publisher insisted she grant at least one interview to a national newspaper. Her book of poems was already a near bestseller. Ned was pleased when the poet chose his Washington paper and surprised when the editor of the book review asked him to come along, sit in on what was likely to be a difficult hour. Difficult but entertaining, the editor added. Gunnar Tribes explained that the poet had an ego the size of the sun itself, and indeed was known informally as the Sun Queen. She was a recluse, loath to interpret her own work or even discuss it. She felt herself to be mistreated and undervalued. This, despite all the honors a poet could want. True, she had yet to receive an invitation from Oslo, and that rankled. She preferred to discuss the appalling conditions in her own country, ruled by thugs and bandits. Gunnar said that Antonia—La Antonia, she called herself—would be impressed if the editor of the newspaper was present at the interview. The poet was a student of hierarchy. The idea that Ned would be in attendance was evidence that things would go smoothly. Respect would be paid.

Gunnar Tribes was a highly respected critic, known to be sympathetic to the dense rhythms of La Antonia. Also, Gunnar was a man of the Left—that was the assurance of her American publisher. Therefore, no Red-baiting. The interview would not stray far from the politics of the hour, the incarcerations, the disappearances—and this put the poet in a good mood. She let it be known that she would tolerate a question or two concerning her verse. Its incendiary effect, its compassion, its woe. Her personal life was strictly off-limits, though it was widely known that, with her companion, she spent most of the year in a rural village, with summer excursions to a seaside villa in Macedonia. La Antonia did have a complicated relationship with the sacred and the profane, poetry and politics. As a woman of the Left she was obliged to enter the realm of the profane. Because it was profane, politics had to be dealt with. Politics had its enlightening aspect, you could say virtue. But politics must not be allowed to contaminate government, a subtle formulation, one not easily grasped. But it seemed, after all, to be a forbidden zone. To say that La Antonia was a difficult interview was to understate the matter. In her poetry the sacred and the profane seemed almost—fungible.

Gunnar Tribes knew what he was up against, but he believed that, properly conducted, the interview would be a newsmaker. He thought it conceivable that Ned Ayres would consent to run it on page one, below the fold of course. What a coup! Ayres had an oddball side and the idea might just appeal to him. But the interview had to stand up, meaning limpid prose with something new in every sentence. Gunnar spent a week boning up, and in due course arrived with Ned Ayres at the poet's suite in the Washington, the hotel across the street from the despised Treasury Department, midwife to so many financial misdeeds. Had this hotel been selected for that reason? A provocation?

La Antonia offered tequila all around and was put out when

Ned and Gunnar declined. The time was eleven a.m. The poet was heard to mutter "Gringos" in a sour voice. The interview proceeded, centered on the poet's new collection, *Walking the Amazon at Twilight*. La Antonia stood at the room's picture window, glaring at the Treasury building, its sullen façade, its many secrets. She wore a gray shirt with gray slacks and a bright red silk scarf. She stood mostly in shadow, but her eyes blazed as she toyed with the curtain string.

Gunnar's questions were subtle yet to the point. La Antonia's gruff answers were transcribed on the critic's yellow legal pad. Gunnar was in his reporter's crouch, head forward, elbows on knees, his questions asked softly and parried by the poet. She was not helpful. There were long silences when the only sound in the room was the ice chips tittering in La Antonia's glass. It was evident that she was fundamentally opposed to discussing her own work. To discuss it was to diminish its value. Poetry existed to be read, not discussed. Now and then she brushed aside a Gunnar question with a look of exasperation. She stared out the window and checked her wristwatch. Ned had difficulty keeping up. His eyelids grew heavy, and when he was on the cusp of sleep he saw Gunnar look up from his yellow legal pad and ask this woman of the Left where politics figured in her work. She was voluble at the many symposia she attended. Havana was a frequent venue. Do you mean the Amazon to suggest the Soviet Union? Politics was central to her work, as central as it was to—Yeats! "What rough beast . . . ," Gunnar said in a whispered voice, as if the reference were unknown to La Antonia. Where did that ideology fit in, exactly? Perhaps I am mistaken here. Did I skip a beat? Would La Antonia enlighten us?

Her head snapped back as if she had been slapped. She opened her mouth but no sound came as she sat glaring at Gunnar, then at Ned, now fully awake. When her voice came it was coarse, a voice from the barrio. Whereas she had been speaking in English, she now spoke in two languages, a kind of shriek, so rapidly Gunnar could not keep up. He translated a fragment for Ned: Fucking Yankee assholes *maricones* morons . . . La Antonia rose from her chair in a fury, arms flailing. And then she was gone. Disappearing into the bedroom where presently came the sound of breaking crockery. The interview had ended.

But Gunnar Tribes was certain he had his knockout. Page one for sure.

Gunnar began to laugh. He said, She was always a pain in the ass. Beloved by the same connoisseurs who value Damien Hirst. A provocateur, Gunnar said. Nothing more. And as has been seen, a colorful vocabulary!

Of course the story got around at once, to much merriment. Gunnar told various versions for the rest of his life. He wrote the interview for the newspaper, a deft piece of destruction. He was certain now of page-one play, but Ned Ayres threatened to kill it unless Gunnar softened the tone, particularly the long paragraph that brought to light La Antonia's "protégé," a boy of eighteen, a young Adonis, Brazilian born. Gunnar reluctantly agreed, but even much softened the piece caused a scandal.

Ned said, You used a hammer to kill a butterfly.

She is not a butterfly, Ned. In her world, she's a giant. We're the butterflies.

With a readership of six hundred thousand, last time I checked.

An ego that big has to be challenged, Gunnar said.

Not necessarily. Or not necessarily by us.

What do you want from the book review? Do we give every loon a pass?

She is not a loon. And her personal life is her own business.

You show up for an interview, you swallow what's given.

She was inarticulate, Ned said. Muddled when she spoke aloud. Her métier is pen and paper. Many people are muddled when discussing something cherished. Deep down they don't want to share it, whatever it is. The interview was a mistake. We should have listened for thirty minutes, then given it up. Thanked her. Walked away. She was way out of her depth. Do you know who she reminded me of, a little? Minus the profanity. Minus the tequila at eleven in the morning. Minus the ability to stay silent. She reminded me of Milo Passarel.

Ned raised his eyebrows and said, She made a mistake. She thought we were her collaborators, present to help her along in a medium she despised. She was naïve. An interview was a rare thing in her life. She distrusted confession, the blade that pierced the veil.

Gunnar rolled his eyes. That's nonsense, Ned.

You didn't get one thing of value from her. She shut up and stayed shut up.

But that's the story, don't you see?

Shooting fish in a barrel, Ned said.

What you say sounds like censorship to me.

I suppose it is. It's called editing.

I can't buy it, Ned.

Some people don't live in the light of day, Ned said. They prefer shadows, a natural habitat. Shadows become them.

What does that mean, Ned?

Ned Ayers waited a moment and then he said, I have some experience with stories like this one.

What do you mean? What experience? Tell me the experience.

You wouldn't understand it. It's on a very different level. A different moment altogether. Sometimes you have to look beyond what's in front of your eyes. Ned looked at Gunnar and gave a wintry smile, evidence of a secret withheld. Ned said, Unforeseen consequences.

That's no help, Ned.

Not to you, Ned replied. Perhaps to me.

He remembered that Gunnar Tribes leaned in, but when he opened his mouth he made no sound. He allowed Ned to have the last word. Fact was, Ned had lost a step. What was he now? Sixty, sixty-five, somewhere in there. Everyone knew that Ned Ayres had no life beyond the paper. In time he would fade away like an old photograph, soft around the edges. In that spirit they left the hotel and walked away in the direction of the newspaper — the plant, as they often called it.

Ned reclined in his Adirondack chair, his remembered dialogue slipping away. Yes, he thought, the dispute with Gunnar Tribes had the makings of a nice cameo in his memoir. Its value was all between the lines.

Ned entertained himself with these memories, evidence that he had led an exciting urban life before retirement drove him to this remote corner of the Eastern Shore, where the pace was glacial. A man had time to think. There was no hurry about anything in Maryland. He was on strange ground. In his lifetime he had mostly traveled east, and now he had nowhere farther to go. He was boxed in, the bay on one side of him and the ocean on the other. Ned Ayres was settled, living out his days. That was it unless he took a slow boat to France or the Low Countries, where he knew a few American expats, or to Spain, where Susan Griffin had retired to a villa in the hilly countryside near Ávila. Someone had told him she was not well, mourning her husband every hour. But Ned was too old for transatlantic voyages regardless of who would be there to greet him. What would he do in Europe? He had a book to write, and Europe was not the place to write it. He wasn't certain that the Eastern Shore was the answer either. One year in and he was still learning about the weather, the wind that spelled trouble and the wind that didn't. In Chicago and Washington he had never thought about the weather. In large cities the weather was an incident. In the country it was ever present. In Herman they thought about the weather from time to time, and in the summer and fall there was always the threat of tornadoes. He looked at the sky, darkening in the northeast. That was one of the bad winds, originating somewhere in the Gulf of Maine. Assisted by a low-pressure zone in the south. Or was that the other way? Well, the bad weather would come or wouldn't come. Nothing to do about it but go inside. He remembered that Elaine was very good with the weather in Chicago, where bad news always came from the north. Lake Michigan was the unlucky lake. Summer in Chicago was miserable. He remembered being goddamned happy when he left for Washington. No one cared about the weather in Washington unless it was a snowstorm that immobilized everything, including traffic. The District of Columbia had no snow-removal equipment. So you sat and stewed until the thaw came. The snap of a tree branch caused him to wheel about, but there was nothing unusual in sight. Ned stared into the woods and then resumed his stroll to the pier and its September breezes. He needed to collect his thoughts.

Ned Ayres was troubled inside his own head, unable to concentrate on the book he was writing. Progress was slow in the beginning and was no better now. The thing seemed to him a jumble and he did not understand why. The objective was simple enough, an account of his life as a newspaper editor, quite straightforward.

But the thread of it kept slipping away, and not for any reason of old age and its discontents, moments of gray confusion, call it chronic forgetfulness. He was taking the project seriously, unlike one close friend who said he should title it *Rat Tales*, ha-ha, amusement he did not join. There had never been a serious book on the craft of editing that went beyond grammar and sourcing and the rest of it found in an introductory course at a school of journalism. Ned Ayres had the idea of devoting a full chapter to the look of page one, the geometry of it, its variety and usefulness and subtle beauty, like a fine landscape, something by Constable or Cézanne. Ned thought there should be mystery also, a problem not quite solved. Page one should be welcoming and surprising at the same time, the lead story something of consequence accompanied by a photograph. An urban story should have the wit and suggestion of something by Kirchner or, rougher still, George Grosz. Provocative, yes, but never a reach beyond the known facts. Always the provocations should lie below the fold, a reminder that the piece was not essential, any more than a fedora was essential to a gentleman crossing Dupont Circle. A beret would do. A Stetson added color. Bareheaded was fine. This was the story of the man who won the lottery and was broke six months later, or the woman racecar driver obliged to quit the track when her eyesight failed. In other words, a slice of life as it was lived. This was partly a matter of space allocation—a one-column head or a two-column head, or if it was placed at the very bottom of the page, a one-line four-column head. A properly edited page one was a thing of beauty that any serious reader would recognize at once and look at it for a minute or so before reading. No tabloid stuff, though. Tabloid material threw the page out of balance because it was contrary to its surroundings, almost surreal—a dirigible tethered to the summit of Mont Sainte-Victoire. And he realized he had taken more than one idea from Milo Passarel. Milo was a defeatist but he was not always wrong. Naturally Ned was unable to entirely reconstruct the paper's page one. Readers did not appreciate innovation, especially those resolute readers who remained on the subscription list. Ned's insight was that beautiful design trumped anything slapped on the Internet. Newspapers now required lean, not fat. Fat was an anachronism, yesterday's virtue, today's sin. After Ned's departure, the new man allowed things to slip back. At the newspaper they called it the Restoration.

Ned had all the research papers that anyone could want, three dozen cartons filled with letters, diaries, notes, fifty-year-old newspaper clippings so brittle they fell apart in your hand. He had stories that no outsider had ever heard, the news behind the news, stories given in the strictest confidence, the teller eager to set the record straight and at the same time imply a particular role at the center of events. This is for you personally, Ned, and if you print one damned word I'll deny it and sue for libel. Later on, when I'm gone, you can do anything you like. Good to have the facts released at last so that people can understand what was at stake and how the secret held after all these years. Won't my kids be surprised! They never had a clue. So many of Ned's confidants were gone now, and the two or three still alive were *non compos mentis*. Care had to be taken so as not to step over the line. The serious editor sought not prurience but enlightenment, always mindful that sometimes only a tissue paper's edge separated the two. But Ned's own material did not gel. It would not *write*. Ned had come to think of himself as an archaeologist assembling fragments of a dead civilization.

After twenty minutes Ned stopped talking to himself and eased out of the Adirondack chair at the edge of the narrow field that rolled down to the bay. The chair was uncomfortable but the espresso warm in the ancient thermos. Watermen were already about, motoring south to the oyster beds and, farther along, the ocean. He could hear very well the soft *put-put*s of the engines. The rising sun cast a sharp glare on the water, so sharp Ned's eyes burned and he had to look away. He wondered whether this place was too quiet for him, too anchored in the past, too removed from the hurly-burly of contemporary life. Hurly-burly was his father's expression. Ned's village, called Rockway, reminded him of Herman, except for the watermen, who were hard cases, most of them. They seemed to be at permanent war with the federal government and the State of Maryland over quotas and other matters relating to the business of commercial fishing. If he nodded at one on the street, he rarely got a nod back. They kept to themselves, the watermen. Ned Ayres had few friends in the village other than the police chief and the mayor. Their lives were so different. The events that had shaped them were wildly different. A life was a story after all, high points and low, high drama or no drama except the cycle of life itself, the interval between birth and the grave. Ned was a public man. His neighbors weren't.

He poured a cup of espresso from the thermos. The month was late September, the year 2005. Ned looked about for his newspaper and realized then that he had forgotten to bring it. The newspaper was lying in the front yard of the manor house and he had missed it entirely. He sat thinking about the house and the newspaper on the lawn and decided he was in a good place. His memoir would take time. He was a patient man and all he needed now was a coherent first chapter. That chapter would unlock the doors to the other chapters. His living situation had been solved at last. He had craved the manor house for all the years he had lived in Washington. He bought it because he could afford it and because it was old and had its own history and would therefore be ideal for the work he had laid out for himself and was now going so badly. He was trying to bring order to the whirl of events and instead he himself was awhirl. In his dark moments Ned had the idea that his editor's life was a curse on what he was called on to do now. Writer's block never occurred to him. In his business, writer's block was something that afflicted poets and novelists and was yet another euphemism for indolence. Moreover, he did not write and had never written. He edited, a higher form altogether. Something ludicrous about it. Ned had been so good with other people's work that he was unable to get on with his own. Put another way, he was the judge parsing the lawyers and now he was obliged to write his own briefs. He sat down again in the Adirondack chair and sipped tepid espresso and concluded that he would have to make a supreme effort. The material was superb but it was a lump of clay, and one fine day he'd look up to discover that it had congealed, as unyielding as a frozen block of gravel.

He looked down at the grass, in shadows away from the water-glare. He saw tiny cobwebs and here and there an insect. The delicate cobwebs reminded him of the veils of the sort women wore years ago. His mother wore a veil when she drove to Muncie for shopping. The veil preserved anonymity and a kind of modesty. But looking at the webs now, Ned was reminded of glass. Transparent. Hard as iron. A shaft of sunlight touched the veils, causing them to collapse and vanish, as if they had never existed or existed only in his memory. Ned dwelled a moment on his veiled mother setting off for Muncie in her Buick, promising to return for dinner. She had a stew on the stove. Don't worry about me, she said, and the bare truth was, no one did. Muncie was an hour or so up the highway. The day was fine. What could go wrong? Of course that was before the Grant business that cast such a pall over Her-

162

man and Herman's surroundings. The trips to Muncie ended and Ned's mother went to Mill City instead, much closer, a rugged city but not dangerous. Ned Ayres heard a creaking and looked up to see a flight of swans. Their wings creaked like a rusty door when they flew. Nasty creatures but beautiful against the azure sky.

Seen from afar, up the narrow carriage path, Ned Ayres's pre–Civil War manor house had the aspect of a Hollywood film set, perhaps one of the strangler films. It was three stories high, built of brick, surrounded by towering black oaks. The house was forever in shade, its great bulk suggesting a fortress or prison. Here and there were flower beds gone to seed. The lawn was overgrown most of the time. The windows of the manor house were opaque, heavy glass distorting the view inside and out. Earl Bosenquet, the hired man, could only do so much. He was old, arthritic, and slow. He talked in a drawling country accent that made him difficult to understand. But Earl was genial most of the time and knew the place, as he said, upwards and backwards. When Ned asked if he could use some assistance, Earl said, Absolutely not under no circumstances, with a vehemence that caused Ned to back off.

Gulls were forever overhead and raccoons roamed the lawn. A derelict turn-of-the-century combine was partly hidden behind one of the oaks, evidence of an attempt at farming once upon a time. The property had been proud and evidently prosperous. The manor house easily accommodated a family of eight or ten. One of the previous owners tried to make it into a rural inn, but that thought was never realized. Any visitor needed a creative imagination to summon the cries of children or the thump of a croquet ball or the swish of a lawn party, the women in crinoline and the men in top hats. Yet surely that was its heritage, gentle and slow-moving, well mannered, without guile. Ned was amused. He thought of his house as a nation gone to seed—badly maintained, inflated, bad vibrations, bad debts, corruption. He thought of Sudan or the Alabama hinterland. And, most recently, the newspaper business.

The house had a history: under the black oak in the side yard was a gravestone, the epitaph effaced after so many years. A stranger wouldn't look at it twice, an anonymous stone, but in the town everyone knew the story. In October of 1862 a deserter from the war arrived at Wilson's Fifty. His arm was in a sling. He was famished and disoriented. He was incoherent, scarcely able to utter an intelligible word. He wore a Confederate gray shirt and Union trousers, and his speech was so garbled it was impossible to know whose army he was part of. He was indisputably a soldier because of the shirt and trousers and the rifle slung over his shoulder. His hands shook. When the doctor came to look him over, he stayed but a half hour, announcing at the end of his examination that the boy was touched in the head, battle fatigue. God knows where he has been, but wherever it was, he's run away from it. Except for the damaged arm the boy had no wounds, or none that were visible. The doctor put his age as between eighteen and twenty. I can't do anything for him, the doctor said, and you can't either. Wilson's wife, Calista, thought of herself as a Christian woman and refused to send the boy away. She put him to bed in one of the second-floor guest rooms and brought him food every morning and evening. The meals were only nibbled at. He began to slip away and in a fortnight he was gone, having managed one clear word before expiring. That word was Antietam. Calista Wilson arranged the funeral and the entire town turned out, since it was impossible to know on whose side the boy fought. The town was equally divided so far as the war was concerned. The minister of the Congregational church conducted the service, ending with a short sermon deploring the loss of life, both sides. The next day Calista Wilson went to the stonemason and requested a marker for the boy's grave. She thought and thought about a suitable epitaph, finally giving it up and requesting merely: An Infantryman Known but to God. For many years schoolchildren came to visit the grave as part of their Civil War lessons, a field trip close to home. Then the school abandoned the Civil War as a separate subject, working it in with the more general American history curriculum. The field trips ended. What was the point? And many of the parents found the effaced gravestone ghoulish, and so grass and thornbush grew around it and the stone sank so that it could hardly be seen. Also, many people thought that the subject of the War Between the States was divisive and often hurtful. Time enough for that at the university. Earl Bosenquet told Ned the story one summer evening, sipping lemonade in the gazebo.

The Wilson family had owned the property for almost a century until the blood ran thin and the money ran out. The grandchildren and their descendants were spendthrift and bad managers generally, a quarrelsome tribe given to dubious experiments. An attempt at cattle ranching had been a failure. Plans to turn the estate into a riding academy foundered. The property decayed and eventually was sold to a newly minted United States senator from the West Coast named Golden, who envisaged it as a weekend retreat. The senator's wife, Henriette, insisted on being put in charge of renovations, and soon enough an invitation to Wilson's Fifty was coveted by friends in Washington and beyond, who saw it as a sort of hybrid of Cliveden, Versailles, and Camp David. Twelve years later, to his great surprise, the senator lost his reelection and in a fury at his ungrateful constituents put the house on the market and announced his decision to relocate to Europe, the Italian Riviera, precisely (he claimed unconvincingly) as "Jack" planned to do had Nixon won in 1960. The hell with them, Jack would've said, meaning the American people. Instead of the American people he would have the grace and favor of Gianni Agnelli and the ambiance of his merry yacht, said to be one hundred and thirty feet in length with ten private staterooms, and a motorboat for water sports and sympathetic companionship in the evenings — so many ports of call in the Adriatic and east to the Aegean. Signore Agnelli was a generous and scrupulous host. No request would go unmet. The senator went on and on about his European plans as Henriette rolled her eyes, one more pipe dream from an overstressed and defeated politician. Moreover, he did not know Signore Agnelli, and Signore Agnelli did not know him. Or me either, Henriette added. But illness intervened and the senator never saw the Adriatic except in his dreams.

There were two more sales after that, and then the property passed into the hands of a Washington lawyer named Fitts, who had the purse to maintain it but not the will or the energy, and so the manor house and its grounds and outbuildings continued their decline—their "desuetude," as the lawyer put it. The fields lay abandoned, overgrown with briarbush. The tennis court and the Summer House were destroyed in a hurricane. The pheasant went away. A coyote showed up now and again to howl at the midnight moon, the ghost of an infuriated Wilson, according to the neighbors. A tragedy, they said, such a fine old place. Do you remember the October afternoon when the president came to lunch? He and Golden were very close friends. But there was nothing to be done about it now. Wilson's Fifty was finished, and nothing short of divine intervention would put it right. The senator was a fool and the lawyer inattentive. Careless was the better word. Those alien to the region did not understand the simple principle of maintenance, a daily business, a full-time job like car-ing for an invalid. One did not advance in such an environment. One *maintained*. One preserved, remained in place, guarded, conscious of the claims of the future. Now, thanks to willful neglect, the property was on life support, not so different from some bankrupt third-world autocracy, the rulers stripping assets as the nation fell to pieces. The local people were quite positive in this view. Fitts died and the estate went on the market once again and was sold at last to the retired newspaper editor who knew it well, having visited often during the senator's reign years before. He and Henriette were especially friendly. Rumor was, they had a walkout, but there was no drama because the senator didn't mind. Earl Bosenquet was asked to verify the rumor but refused to say one word. The editor paid him well. He was owed respect.

Ned Ayres had fallen at once for the manor house and its surroundings, as another man might fall for a starlet or the roulette wheel, perhaps a racehorse or an Old Master. Ned had his eyes on the place from the beginning. He was young then but foresaw the day when he would retire like a good American and work on his memoirs. He saw the memoirs as his life's work, occupying his time as—had things turned out differently—grandchildren might. Or his golf game. Or taking an annual cruise, the Caribbean or the Baltic. Shuffleboard in the afternoon and too much whiskey at night. Not likely. He had intended all along to work at a deliberate pace, but now he was inert. When one had spent a working lifetime attempting to understand the motives of others—well, you came up dry when writing of your own. Pleasures and miseries, they too were dimly seen. What was not dimly seen was the ambiance of the newsroom, the swing of it, the excitement when presented with something utterly unexpected. An Oval Office scandal, a cabinet secretary caught in flagrante, the suicide of a revered jurist, stories that went on for months and were rarely resolved to everyone's satisfaction. Pieces of the story were missing, lost, hidden away, a general silence on the part of those who knew him—rarely her—and the situation. At such times a newspaper reporter could believe that the city of Washington was a place of dark corners, inaccessible, abnormal, mysterious. Ned Ayres had his diaries and notebooks and the rest, the cartons meticulously dated and organized by subject, observations on American journalism, its ethics and personalities, its rituals, the milieu of the newsroom, ending when he walked out the door, the paper under his arm, its headline immaculate: BUSH DEFEATS KERRY. And so at long last he had a congenial place of his own to write. No distractions.

Of course Ned had too much house, he knew that. Three stories and fifteen rooms, most of it in one stage or another of disrepair. The roof leaked. The furnace needed attention. The interior was filthy and small things were out of order. The centerpiece of the fanlight above the front door was cracked. Editor Ayres had drastically underestimated the cost of mere maintenance, he who had run such a tight newsroom and had been so careful when line-editing a piece for the paper. He had badly needed a change of scene, and the manor house held wonderful memories for him and a provocative history that went back before the Civil War. At the end of his life Edgar Allan Poe had rusticated for a spell in one of the third-floor bedrooms, a servant's room actually, drying out from his usual excess. He had left a fragment of a poem, the handwriting all but indecipherable but unmistakably Poe's own hand. A century later Mencken was a frequent visitor. A framed photograph of the blue-eyed sage hung in the library, its inscription to a certain Jane Irma Smith: "Get out of Paris as soon as you can. It is poison to Americans." Poe's poem and Mencken's photo with its two-sentence admonition were placed either side of a sketch by the Frisian artist Lawrence Alma-Tadema, two Roman boys hauling water from a well. Ned noticed at once that the poem, the letter, and the sketch were screwed into the wall. They were not meant to be removed, as much a part of the manor house as the fireplace near the piano and the vast library, two stories high with a teak ladder attached to a rail in the ceiling.

The library contained more than two thousand volumes, mostly a legacy of the Wilson years. Lawyer Fitts and the senator's wife were avid readers and pleased to find that a number of the volumes were signed. James Branch Cabell. Ida Tarbel. Alice Roosevelt Longworth had supposedly called the library "the greatest room in the East," certainly greater in every way than the mundane Oval Office or the overdecorated Blue Room in the White House, where the only books were ceremonial. Everyone gathered in the library for drinks. Senator Lester Golden and his wife were enthusiastic hosts with a wide circle of friends, so the evenings were animated, the conversation wide-ranging with, most often, a political undertow. The Remarques. John Gunther. William O. Douglas. Gregory Peck. Alger Hiss, a quiet presence, but when he spoke the table fell silent. Henriette Golden valued friendship above all else. She was a sparkling Californian, a daughter of the entertainment industry, her father a producer and her mother an actress who shined brightly for a decade and then retired to look after her husband, "keeping an eye on him," as she put it. Henriette was a thoughtful hostess who set an immaculate table. She was keen for gossip and usually placed Ned Ayres on her left, Ned a good listener, attentive to nuance and up to speed on the ways and byways of the capital. In other words, he had something to contribute. Henriette was amused when Ned declared that the thing about Washington was that you had to know whose hand was on whose leg and whether that hand signified a proposal of marriage or something else. The capital was alive with the sound of intrigue. Henriette saw at once that Ned was one of them, a value-added addition to the table—and all this time she had found the news business a forbidden zone, utterly baffling, as if it were a kind of cult with its own rituals and sacred texts, passwords, goes and no-goes. Bottom line: the press could not be trusted. This Ned was cut from different cloth, cloth that resembled her own.

Ned's memories of the Saturday-night suppers were fond and he intended to devote a full chapter to them, who was at table and what was said and the menus and the parlor games later. What Hiss said to Gunther and what Gunther said back. The real attraction to the Golden table was its conversation, the less circumspect the better. True coin was indiscretion. In the beginning Ned found himself conflicted over just how much he committed to the pages of the slender, green leather diary he had bought at Mark Cross for the occasion, not a word transcribed until he was safely upstairs and abed. He took the precaution of writing in code. He did expect that the guests along with the senator would be dead before it came time to write anything. Ned was usually the youngest guest in the room by thirty years and more, except for Henriette. Also, there remained the question of how much privacy was allowed around a dinner table, with its exaggeration and presumption, some malice, sly references. The dead could not be libeled as a matter of law. As a matter of personal ethics, there were the usual disputes. What was the shelf life of a reputation?

He did promise himself to leave his work at the office. Milo Passarel had said something about it, to the effect that dinner at the Goldens' was not a news conference. Of course the divide was not entirely clear. The line between work and pleasure was not clear. Ned never used the dinners at the Goldens' to advance a story. The arguments and jokes were irresistible but plainly for another day. It was in the dining room of the manor house that he first heard of the liaison between Mrs. Kennedy and the dissolute Onassis. He had done nothing with it. He had never edited anything concerning Mrs. Kennedy, who deserved all the privacy she could get. And here, it had to be admitted, Ned Ayres's memory did a little congratulatory jig.

Milo Passarel had introduced Ned to the Goldens. I know you to be a man of discretion, Ned. Things can get—a little rowdy at the Goldens'. Nothing serious but there's a lot of gossip, most of it bogus in my view. But the company is most unusual, always someone there you've wanted to meet but never had the opportunity. Milo smiled, almost paternally, Ned thought. When you get the invitation, Milo said, accept it. See what happens.

The first time he entered the library Ned was enchanted. The books, the Alma-Tadema sketch of the Roman boys at the well, slight as it was, a masterpiece all the same, and nicely situated between the Poe and the Mencken. As if to add a touch of the occult, a Ouija board rested on a nearby card table, complementing in some strange way the Alma-Tadema and the Poe. Ned was greeted cordially as a particular friend of the publisher and his wife, known for their discretion and amiability. He was welcomed into whatever conversation was on offer, the ever-mediocre state of the National Symphony Orchestra, the plight of the captive nations of eastern Europe, the extraordinary *Lear* playing off-Broadway in New York. Are you a theater man, Ned? Have you seen it? You must. It's a miracle! Ned specifically recalled the many discussions of firearms, the over-and-under versus the side-by-side, the merits of the Browning as opposed to the Purdey or the Boss. Beautiful balance, the Boss. Light as a violin. They were priming themselves for the duck blinds in the morning, five a.m. sharp. At the ding of a chime the party would dissolve into the dining room, a moment of confusion as the place cards were examined. Conversation was initiated by the senator, everyone expected to contribute, domestic politics first, foreign policy to follow, a senatorial monologue, a *tour d'horizon;* his table, his subjects, while Milly Bosenquet, Earl's daughter, served the crab bisque. After twenty minutes of *tour d'horizon* the table more or less broke into several groups, each with its own topic.

Henriette would turn to Ned and quietly commence a reminiscence of her youth in Beverly Hills and the scandals of the film community, so much riper than now, or her year abroad when she was twenty-one, an invitation from Milo and Lana Passarel to visit them at their villa near Granada. She was invited for a weekend but stayed for a week at their insistence. That was the beginning of her love affair with the Spanish language, the corrida, and the poems of García Lorca. Dinner never began before ten p.m. On her last day with the Passarels she met a boy and they went off for a week together to Galicia, in the west of the country. When Henriette hesitated a moment, Ned urged her to continue. He had never visited Spain and was eager to learn about it. And the Passarels. How was life at the villa? But Henriette only smiled and said that Milo and Lana were very private people, the villa a kind of sanctuary. She smiled. No raised voices. They were wonderful hosts and sad when she departed with her señorito, who had never traveled to the Spanish west and was eager to see it, Spain's neglected region, so dour and unforgiving, the people hard as tree bark. Franco was feared and revered as savior of the nation. No one spoke of the war, and if you brought it up they changed the subject. It is not your affair, señorita. The war was a family matter, in the way of being a family secret, their national calamity. However, the Reds were finished as a national party. So there was some good after all. The boy was an aristo and wouldn't talk about it either, except to say that Franco was misunderstood by the outside world, particularly by France and the United States. Britain. When in Spain it was not correct to speak of the war. The war was settled history. Stare decisis.

Ned Ayres listened with care. Henriette spoke with ardor, her eyes glittering, her speech rapid. It was as if she were describing a ballet or a great European novel, sublime but difficult of entry. You had to have been there.

Anyhow, she said, a great adventure.

Ned said, Sounds like it, and more.

Have you been abroad?

Never, he said.

Any plans?

No, he said.

Ned, that's appalling.

Ned said, I'm trying to run a newspaper.

Is a trip to Spain or France disqualifying? She heard her name and looked up, Lester waving from the other end of the table.

Ned glanced around the room, soft in candlelight. Milly Bosenquet drifted among the diners, a bottle of wine in each hand. Ned knew it was time for the table to turn but he was in thrall to Henriette, and she seemed not to mind that their end of the table remained frozen. The others were arguing about the coming election.

So I didn't learn anything about the Spanish war, Henriette said, except that no one wanted to talk about it, and I suppose that's knowledge of a sort. So we spent five days in Galicia. La Coruña, then Vigo.

What's Vigo? Ned asked.

Clapped-out seaport, Henriette said.

A random destination, Ned said.

Not quite, Henriette said. It was fated, I think. Plus, everyone needs a Vigo. You should know that, Ned. Vigo's a place on the map, come upon by surprise, stay awhile and never go back. When you're there, no one knows who you are. They don't care who you are. The chances are slim to none that you'll meet anyone you know. It's not a tourist destination, Neddy. There's nothing in Vigo that a tourist would wish to see. We had a room on the top floor of a hotel overlooking the harbor. Not swank but clean. Nice view if you like maritime views. I remember a small bar in the lobby, three stools and a selection of sherries and red wines, local brandy if you could stand it. The desk clerk was rude, offended I think because Fernando and I were obviously together and just as obviously not married. Marriage mattered to them in Galicia because in those days the region was traditional. Strait-laced when it came to dirty weekends and foreigners. And I doubt if anything's changed from then to now. The desk clerk seemed not at all impressed by Fernando's lispy Castilian accent and his black beret. He was tall and slender, Fernando. And looked down on people, literally. The desk clerk's manner suggested that I was not suitable, an American adventuress chasing after a *conde* with a fancy surname—

So you were chasing him, Ned said.

Definitely, Henriette said. Fernando found it all amusing until suddenly he didn't find it amusing. He was bored. Thing about aristos is that they're frequently bored. Don't you agree?

Every time, Ned said.

Fernando gave the desk clerk a look that put an end to it, Henriette said. He rather wilted before our eyes and turned his back as we stepped to the elevator with our bags, my one and his two. Later on we found a good fish restaurant in the harbor. After midnight we heard some pretty good Gypsy music and things loosened up a little, not much. Fernando played the guitar for them and earned a good round of applause. I was so surprised. I didn't know he played the guitar. Truth was, I didn't know much about him at all. His family had apartments in Madrid and Majorca and an estate in Catalonia. That ever happen to you, Ned? Become involved with a girl and realize after a few dates that you know nothing about her? Henriette paused there, not waiting for an answer but seemingly way back in her memory as she toyed with her butter knife.

All the time, Ned said untruthfully, wanting only to show solidarity. He thought he saw tears in Henriette's eyes but that could have been the candlelight. Around them the table was aroar with conversation. An argument had broken out between the Maryland governor and Alger Hiss, something to do with a grammar school they had both attended in Baltimore. They had different memories of the headmaster. Alger had raised his voice, something he rarely did. As he talked he drummed his fingers on the tablecloth. Henriette listened to them a moment and then with a puzzled shake of her head turned back to Ned. She said, Thing about Vigo, Neddy, is that it's not any place you'd choose to go to. You arrive there for the night because there's nowhere else. Santiago de Compostela is too far away when it's eight o'clock at night and you're starving because you've been driving all day long and haven't had anything to eat since breakfast and the man you're with has been silent for most of that time. So you take what's available and stay for two days and two nights, and once you leave you never return. Not random, Ned. Fated.

Even so, you remember quite a lot.

I do, don't I, she said.

And it was a long time ago.

Yes, she said. A while back.

I'm not so sure I like your aristo.

Probably you wouldn't. He was an acquired taste. Very sure of himself.

I can't say I've ever met one, Ned said. But I wonder. If you've met one, have you met them all?

Henriette thought a moment. No, she said.

You probably met them growing up in Malibu.

Beverly Hills, she said. I think there was one, maybe two. In the film business. Also, there was a countess. She worked in wardrobe. There was a rumor she was born in Oklahoma, but nobody minded. She looked like a countess, tall with straight black hair. The Habsburg lip, someone said. Anyhow, she was just a wardrobe girl.

Another reinvention, Ned said.

I suppose, Henriette agreed. And you, Ned? Met many reinventions?

More than I can count, Ned said.

The business you're in, Henriette began.

Actually, Ned said, there's not much room for reinvention in the newspaper business. The task is to discover other people's reinventions. The results are not always successful. Ned heard something in his voice and took a swallow of wine. He looked at her directly and said, I had a girlfriend called Elaine. We were going to be married but she didn't like my business. She thought it led to self-absorption, meaning there was no room in it for anyone else. And he told Henriette the story, ending with the long cable, the one that was nearly incoherent, though not so incoherent that something wouldn't be made of it. He said, She died in Africa.

I'm sorry, Henriette said.

It was a while ago.

So many things are, Henriette said with a wan smile.

We were great with each other for a year or more. But she didn't like my business.

It wasn't you. It was business?

Me *in* the business, I think.

Why didn't you leave the business?

It was my métier. Still is. I was fully invested.

Was she the last serious girlfriend?

There have been others. Elaine always cast a shadow.

Long shadow, sounds like.

Ned nodded. Someone made a joke and the table was wrapped in laughter.

Ned said, So you were never tempted to return to Vigo?

Go back to Vigo? Never. What would be the point?

I don't know, Ned said. See if it's changed?

Vigo will never change, Henriette said.

And the Spanish boy, Ned said, the aristo so fluent at Gypsy guitar. What about him? Do you suppose he ever went back? Returned for old times' sake? Look into the hotel bar to see if there were still three stools? Ned already had a sense of the Spaniard's looks and bearing, the boy conquistador, probably a sixteenth-century face to go with the title, complete with a mustache and a tin helmet.

Are you jealous, Neddy? You sound jealous.

Ned opened his mouth to issue a denial, then laughed instead. He said, Probably.

No need, Henriette said. That's the end of the story.

Not the end if Fernando went back.

I doubt it, Henriette said. Though how can I be sure? Fernando was a sentimentalist, it's true. More than I am. Was. Who saw himself as a kind of vagabond cavalier, so maybe he did, later on when he was married to his contessa and in charge of the family estates. Did I mention that his family owned land in Galicia? We did not stop to visit the property and, truthfully, I'm not sure he knew exactly where it was. We stayed in touch for a while and then I stopped writing. When I stopped, so did he. I did notice his name in the papers a few years ago. He was working for the government, an ambassador somewhere. Don't tell me you've never had a Vigo, Neddy.

Not one like yours, Ned said.

You've missed out, then.

So far, anyway, Ned said.

I've never told that story to anyone. Not a living soul.

It's safe with me, Ned said.

Well, let me know when she comes along and we'll have a dinner in her honor. I'll seat her next to Alger.

Is that a promise?

I never lie, Henriette said.

Ned Ayres looked around the room. He and Henriette were the only ones under sixty years old. The room was drenched in nostalgia, and to understand the nostalgia you had to be of that age and of that ilk, remembering the French foreign minister who said this and the Russian spy who did that until he was unmasked by the sly woman seated next to Senator Golden, the one with her hair in a tight bun and already smoking a cigarillo, though the table was not cleared. Dessert was on the way. The truth was, this was a room full of secrets, many of them decades old. Most of the secrets remained secrets; at least they had not been fully told. They were a kind of coin of the realm and nonnegotiable. Ned was mostly in the dark as to the provenance of the coins. Ned imagined Elaine on the senator's left, leaning in, trying to hear the payoff. Often the payoffs were themselves obscure; and for some unknown reason Ned remembered the British correspondent at William Grant's funeral, nicely turned out in a bespoke suit and a Bailey hat. He had covered the Battle of the Somme and for that reason or some other reason was leaning heavily on a cane. He would have fit wonderfully at Henriette's long table. He had beautiful manners and had been everywhere. He and Elaine would have gotten on well together so long as the Brit did not mention the Somme. Elaine had no interest in war stories. Politics bored her. Ned looked again at the woman with the hair bun and the cigarillo, smiling now at some story the senator was telling. Poor Elaine would not have been au courant. The names and places would fly by unacknowledged. She would think she was in a madhouse or a sinister menagerie. Ned caught some of the senator's words: Vienna, Owen Lattimore, "Beetle" Smith, Edward Stettinius, *Open City*, Oak Ridge.

The table had turned decisively, and Ned made a comment to the woman on his left, straining to read her place card and failing because the card lay face-down. Without preamble she began to talk about her father, a writer of luminous reputation. She spoke touchingly of her father's last years, disappointments and an unruly death. But his books were still in print and that was the important thing, because if they were in print, so, in a sense, was he. She reached beyond Ned to look at his place card. She said, So, Ned Ayres, what do you do?

Newspaper editor, Ned said.

Are you discreet, then?

Most of the time, Ned said.

And your father, what did he do?

He is a judge, Ned said.

A judge! Where from? Is he on the Supreme Court?

He is a circuit judge in Indiana. Herman. A small town.

Where is it? I've heard the name before.

Near Muncie, Ned said.

That character on the radio. Did he not speak about Herman? Herrrrrrman. A radio program.

Ed Watts, Ned said.

Who is that?

The radio man. His name is Ed Watts, earned his living by making a joke of Herman. A town of dullards and no-accounts. But it's really just a small town like any other.

So we say good riddance to Ed Watts.

Definitely, Ned said.

I've never been to Indiana. I've never been anywhere in the Midwest, except once to Chicago. Nothing ever brought me to the Midwest. It's terra incognita to me. Isn't that a shame. I grew up here and there, New York, Paris for a while after the war. I married an unsuitable man, and when he left I moved from London to Washington. It's where many of my schoolgirl friends live. Now I live near the Goldens in Cleveland Park. I like them both, but my hunch is that Lester will not be with us much longer. I fear he will lose his election. He is not popular in California. Henriette will be crushed.

She will?

Definitely.

Ned's attention strayed, an argument at the other end of the table. He did not catch the drift. He did notice Alger Hiss smiling. Hiss was not part of the argument but he seemed to be enjoying it.

Ned said, Lester will lose? How do you know that?

She said, Because I know the woman who's going to defeat him. Lester has not been attending to business.

Does he know? Shouldn't he be warned? Ned was smiling.

He won't listen to the people who know.

And with that, the table began to empty. Soon Ned was sitting alone. The others were settling in at the card tables. Two tables of bridge, as it turned out, and one of poker. Ned was the odd man who played neither bridge nor poker, so he refilled his glass and slipped away to the window seat next to the piano, noting, not for the first time, that the poker table was raucous while the bridge tables were dead silent except for the murmured bids. Three hearts. One no trump. Two civilizations, Ned thought, fundamentally incompatible. The senator had offered Ned his place at the bridge table but Ned demurred. The ambiance was pleasant enough, watching the players in their various ways of concentrating, the clatter of chips as the antes were raised and raised again. Alger Hiss sat straight up like a schoolboy asked to read a text, *Moby-Dick* perhaps, or *Lord Jim*. Hiss held his cards in both hands as one might hold a Bible. The man himself was mute, his eyes narrowed, his face disclosing nothing of importance. On those hands that were beyond him, he said quietly, I'm out, and collected his busted cards with infinite patience and placed them close to the gathering pile of chips. Perhaps then an inward sigh as he watched the end of the play, when Senator Golden was called and he revealed a full house, tens with aces up. Groans around the table except for Alger Hiss, who offered a second's worth of smile. Meanwhile, the bridge tables pressed silently on. From time to time Hiss glanced in the direction of the bridge tables, so quiet, a concentration of forces. Ned watched all this, an evening's pantomime, the air — Ned thought the air was thin. Then Henriette was at Ned's side, having returned from the kitchen. She insisted on helping Milly Bosenquet with the cleanup.

They sat in silence, watching the tables, until Ned said, Tell me one thing. What was the name of the hotel?

Henriette laughed. The Grande, she said, and added after a

181

moment's pause, I doubt if Fernando ever returned to Vigo. It was not his sort of town. He felt superior to it. Also, he liked Franco but didn't like Franco's entourage. Brutes, he called them. Riffraff. Nevertheless, according to Fernando, Spain required a strong-man. The population had—energetic appetites that were better off contained. They had a natural dignity. I would say a highly developed sense of self that had to be respected, except, of course, for the Reds among them. Red was not Catholic. Red was not Spain. The Reds suffered terribly after the war, so many atrocities to be counted and avenged. And the fascists had the upper hand. I don't think Spain's environment was good for women. I don't mean bed necessarily. I mean daily things, the way men and women get on together hour to hour. Do you see what I'm saying, Ned? Something strict about them. And dignity has its limits. It must never seem forced. How old are you, Ned?

He said, Thirty, give or take.

You should have a girlfriend. Then, when you come here for the weekend, she could come with.

Ned said, I had a steady girlfriend but she went away. One afternoon she was there and the next she was gone.

Headstrong, Henrietta said.

Headstrong, Ned agreed.

Was it a grand affair?

It was while it lasted.

And what became of her? God, Ned, it's like pulling teeth talking to you.

She was the one who died, Ned said.

Lord, Henriette said. I put my foot in it again. I'm sorry.

She died abroad of an illness, Ned said. Before she died she wrote a conciliatory message. I guess you could call it a mea culpa. She had become bewitched by Africa and its wildlife, its dusks and dawns. She thought we should give our romance one more try but in her heart I believe she knew that I was already taken. Unavailable because of my work. That's not quite right. I was available but only at my own convenience. All those late nights, erratic hours generally. The scent of a story that could send you around the bend, a dog worrying a bone so that you follow the damned dog wherever it leads. It's important. The dog is more important than you are, so you pay attention to the dog.

Ned said, Newsman died the other day in Moscow, where he had lived and reported for decades. Charming man, great raconteur. Can you imagine it? Year after year, one autocrat following another. Your telephone tapped as a matter of course. Your mail opened. Your sex life examined minutely. Newsman was meticulous. Nothing escaped his attention. He continued to look for the story that would explain it all, a story as powerful as anything Dostoyevsky wrote. But he was not Dostoyevsky, so none did. But he continued the chase. He did this every day for decades. One wife left him and the second wife left him, too. He was bereft both times, but not so bereft that he missed the evening briefing delivered by a lad who was young enough to be his grandson. By that time he was married yet again, this time to a magazine correspondent. But they quarreled and she moved out, the last slam of the door for him. He knew Stalin, you know, Ned said. It's fair to say not well. No one knew Stalin well except possibly his daughter. And Stalin knew him. Stalin was convinced that Newsman was a spy sent by the American authorities to undermine him. This was lunatic. Newsman's Stalin obsession was his own. No one attempted to undermine Stalin without paying a price. But our man in Moscow continued his search. Chasing Stalin had become his life's work, and it's fair to say that after all these years Newsman and story became one. There was no difference between them.

He spoke the language beautifully. He roamed the Soviet empire, disappearing for weeks at a time, always carrying his bookbag of Russian stories, Gogol, Pushkin, Babel. And on one of his excursions he vanished, no one knew where. The Gulag, perhaps, or an accident. An entrapment? Perhaps that. Newsman's health was precarious, so a heart attack or stroke could not be ruled out. His friends in the international press corps were convinced that Stalin had exacted his own revenge, the tyrant's hand reaching from the grave, a coarse voice issuing instructions. In any case, Newsman was never heard from again. Left behind were dispatches, forty years' worth, wedged into a steamer trunk in his apartment near the Arbat. One of his friends tried to interest Harvard, but no one at Harvard seemed interested. Steamer trunk? Dispatches, most of them falling apart inside the trunk? Termites? Thanks but no thanks. Someone thought of making an approach to the CIA, but that idea went nowhere. Claude was naturally suspicious of the security services. And so the steamer trunk remained in situ until one day it vanished, no one knew where. At that time the apartment was occupied by one of his ex-wives.

All right, Ned said, An extreme case, I admit. An obsessive personality found in many lines of work, the law and banking, professional sports, the theater, professional gambling. Difference is, a reporter like Claude is a kind of poet, many of his insights found between the lines of his dispatches. His material resisted clarity. In fact, his work was dangerous. Claude was a chatterbox, though when the talk turned to methods and sources, he fell silent. Also, he was a Johnny one-note and by no means a celebrity reporter. His clients were few: two newspapers in Michigan, one in upstate New York, another in New Mexico. Honolulu as well. The editors of these papers had never met Claude, who seldom traveled abroad. "Abroad" to him meant North America. His copy might as well have been labeled: For Connoisseurs Only.

By the way, he was a slender man and barely five feet tall, always moving at a brisk trot. His wives conceded that he was a considerate lover, though tireless.

Everyone liked him, Ned said.

But they didn't want to *be* him, if you see what I mean.

To which Henriette raised her eyebrows and smiled.

Ned Ayres retired early that night, not without a last look at Alger Hiss, who seemed not to have moved a muscle in the past hour. He continued to sit ramrod straight and silent, unless he was calling, raising, or folding, his voice coming from the deep pocket inside his head. He had accumulated an impressive pile of chips and yet his expression remained the same. Ned thought his mind was elsewhere, incarcerated in past time. He was chronically short of money, so his poker winnings were helpful. It was clear to Ned that he was in the game for the long haul, whatever it took. Watching Hiss, Ned was reminded of someone else, he couldn't think who. Then it came to him, not who, but what. Ned was reminded of a great actor, minimal lines, minimal movements, an actor's "business." In that way he seemed to hover above the table, a kind of ghost. He had a reputation for intellectual brilliance but that was not what Ned saw. He saw cunning.

Henriette had long since said good night. Now Ned slowly mounted the stairs to his third-floor bedroom, called the Poe Room for its sometime inhabitant. He lay down on the bed at once and began to make notes of the evening, the jokes, the presence of Hiss, Henriette's Vigo excitement. At a distant sound he put his pen and diary aside and waited. He turned off the bedside light.

In a moment Henriette glided into the room. Ned made room for her on the bed. She whispered something about Poe's ghost, present but unseen. She went on to recite a stanza of "Ulalume," grinning all the while. She said, He is thought to have written his poems in this very room, composing at night when his nerves settled. It's a nice room, isn't it? I like to think that Poe wrote at night when the house was silent. His mind was not silent. Nice to imagine also that in summer the black bats came and went. They do now. Henriette scratched Ned's foot with her toenail and apologized. Poe made her do it. Poe supervised the room. It was his room after all and God knows how many nightmares he endured in his narrow bed, alone but for the racket within. Maybe he wasn't always alone. Maybe there was company. I prefer that, don't you, Ned? Henriette shivered slightly, another reminder. Her voice was soft.

When she asked Ned if he believed in ghosts, he said he did. He said he imagined all the people he had known well gathered in one room, waiting for his arrival when the time came. Welcoming me home, Ned added. No hard feelings. No scores settled or even hinted at. A general amnesty for mistakes made, however grave. He wrapped a lock of her hair around his finger and tugged gently. She asked if he would tell her a story, a short one. So he told her a story about Poe and his many liaisons with women. It was made up. He had no idea of Poe's life except for its turbulence, how it began and how it ended. Henriette sighed with pleasure because the story ended well, a happy ending, Poe in a state of bliss. He had looked for it all his life and now he had found it, his Eastern Shore. He could go no farther. The world he had known ended there.

But Henriette had misunderstood.

You look gloomy, she said. Shall I tempt you from your gloom? They rolled together in Poe's disheveled bed, in shadows from the light of a half moon, a rocking-chair moon. They went on and on, and when they were done the moon was out of sight in the western sky. Henriette sighed and spoke a few words into Ned's ear. She must go. She had stayed longer than she intended. She searched for her slippers, then remembered she had come barefoot. Ulalume would be a barefoot girl ... Ned lay on his back listening to Henriette. She slipped from the room as easily as she had slipped into it. Ned heard the creak of the staircase, then silence. He stepped to the window and looked out. A light breeze had come up, so weightless, random, he could not sense its direction. Ned realized then that he was slick with sweat, his own and hers, too. The night air was cool but he was sweating all the same. Ned lit a cigarette, whistling the tobacco smoke though his teeth, the smoke hanging in a cloud before drifting slowly to the open window, where it hung before dissolving into the Maryland darkness. A sliver of light was visible to the east, a waterman homeward bound, his engine barely audible. An early hour even for watermen, so perhaps he carried contraband. Nothing much was audible in the manor house. Ned wondered if this room, Poe's room, was Henriette's designated assignation place. She certainly knew her way around in the dark. Probably the Eastern Shore was her American Vigo. And now it could be his, too, for this one night and other nights to come. Ned closed his eyes and imagined himself as master of the manor house and all that went with it, including the myths. Perhaps he would write a book there sometime in the far distant future. If Henriette was to be believed, Poe's spirit could be summoned at will. She did not explain how one went about that, the summoning. He had no reason to doubt Edgar Allan Poe's spectral presence. There was the evidence of the poem and the room itself, Poe-sized and dark. Still, the stories were well worn — Poe wandering through the gardens at midnight, Poe disappearing into the village and returning half clothed, Poe howling at the moon. The stories had been handed down, buffed and elaborated by a hundred retellings, a myth of the region. There seemed to be no reason to doubt Poe's occupancy of the third-floor bedroom.

Ned listened to the waterman's boat recede, its engines withering away into silence. He himself could buy a boat, a small one with a sail and an outboard engine. He had never skippered a boat, but Earl Bosenquet could give him lessons. How to tack. How to come about. The meaning of the ominous and rare southeast wind. He would give house parties once a month, always with a mystery guest like Alger Hiss. Ned Ayres lit another cigarette. Now the outdoor silence was complete and unnerving, too. He had stepped away from his normal sphere. He preferred cities with their ambulance sirens and three a.m. laughter and a newspaper to set the day's context. Retirement was years off and Ned was a present-moment man, though it was fair to surmise that today's moment was very like yesterday's. They were kin. That was the way personal history worked out, or a town's history or a nation's. Everyone lived to the tick of a clock. There was little sense in trying to imagine the future. He supposed he could continue with his bachelor's life, now as natural as his flat Indiana accent and his size-twelve shoes and, more to the point, his twelve-hour workdays. His world was the office. He had had a dozen Vigos in his life and none of them were in Spain. If your passion was news, you need never dine alone. Ned Ayres stood at the open window a very long time, and when the wind shifted he heard, far away, the ding of a buoy bell.

Two years later Lester Golden lost his Senate seat, and he and Henriette departed Washington and the Eastern Shore for Beverly Hills. In due course the property passed into the hands of the lawyer Fitts, who held on as long as he could until his nerves broke down, just a year before Ned Ayres bought it and began his extensive repairs. He and Henriette maintained a correspondence for a year or so and then the correspondence languished. Reading between the lines, not at all difficult to do, Ned concluded that Henriette had a new boyfriend. In any case, Lester was ill and failing.

Ned phoned once to ask Henriette if she would ever return to the East, and she said probably not. Washington's a place to which, once you've left, you rarely return. Washington changes colors, so many people moving in and out. Good ones, too. Charming when they choose to be. Lester's finished there. So am I. What's there for me?

Me, Ned said with a laugh.

We had our fling, she said. Good fling, too, and longer than most. But it's old news. It's history.

Understood, Ned said. A pity all the same.

It's in the past. We're in retreat.

The past with a happy edge, Ned said. We had good times.

Conceded, Henriette said.

Why, when we were rolling around on that third-floor bed even Poe got up to dance.

Let it rest, she said. We're too much alike, Ned.

I don't think so, Ned said.

Then you haven't been listening. You always said you were a good listener.

I'm a hell of a good listener.

I am with another, she said, her voice rising.

Already? he said. I had no idea.

Yes, she said.

Often when a conversation went off the rails Ned introduced a fresh thought, what he called a spinner. He said, When you're in

Washington, give me a call. We can dine together. Catch up with each other, nothing more than that—

But Henriette had already rung off.

What on earth was she talking about? They were not the least bit alike. They were as unalike as Beverly Hills and Herman, but that did not mean they could not get on. He had thought of them as an expressionist painting, clashing colors but harmonious the longer you looked at it. "I am with another," such an archaic phrase. The phrase was unworthy of her. So they were quits. Ned would miss her company, her anecdotes of life in Southern California and enigmatic Vigo, her easy ways of lovemaking. She had led an interesting life. She told a good story. She had a light touch and a beautiful smile. She traded back tales of the capital, but in time it was clear she trusted her own stories more than she trusted Ned's stories. She had never taken Washington seriously, a city that made even Los Angeles seem self-effacing. She was there because Lester was there, a senator at last. He had always wanted to be one. But that was finished now. She did not believe the newspaper either, so leaden, so without humor. This became clear as the romance rolled along and then fell to pieces and finally came to an end with her harsh word, "Conceded."

Ned did not know it then, but Henriette was his last serious love affair, meaning one that had legs, here today and here tomorrow. He believed now that it was time for a change, so he put the Dupont Circle apartment on the market and went in search of a house, perhaps something in nearby Georgetown within walking distance of the office. His own gait was slow motion and, by and by, Ned began to think of retirement, though not in any self-conscious way. Time seemed to accumulate, so much garbage. The business side of the paper became ever more intrusive. Milo Passarel's mood darkened. The newsroom budget was cut and cut again. Ned promised Milo he would make do with less. The mood in the newsroom soured and a number of the senior reporters took early buyouts and moved away to be close to their children and grandchildren. And in due course Ned followed them out the door. He left a typewriter behind as a memento, but the new man disposed of it at once. The Smithsonian was happy to have it, a Ned Ayres original. Royal by marque. The new man believed there was altogether too much nostalgia in his newsroom. He wanted things forward-looking, tomorrow's technology, strictly up to date and beyond.

Seven

FERRIS WHEEL

NED'S OWN LIFE on the Eastern Shore no longer included Washington, a marathon drive for a man his age.
He was now close to eighty years old with failing eyesight. Ned returned to Washington a few times, taking the bus
from one of the Maryland towns and returning the same way.
Once he stayed with friends, twice at the Willard. So many good
friends were gone or ailing. He paid one visit to the newspaper office, the paper struggling now. Milo Passarel had sold it at an ad-
vantageous moment and was said to be living happily in his villa
near the Alhambra, his extended family installed nearby. Milo was
near ninety and Lana was dead, her ashes spread over the pretty
garden that caught the morning sun. Susan Griffin was dead. Ned
had sent a note to Milo on learning of Lana's death and received a
postcard in return, Milo's jerky handwriting all but indecipherable.
On reading about Ned's memoir-in-progress his script firmed up:
Keep me out of it. Ned was pleased to find his own name still on
the masthead of the newspaper, along with four predecessors and
the short-lived successor. At an appalling cost Ned received the
paper daily by mail, so he was able to keep up with the changes
—not that he understood the precise nature of the changes, since
they were announced in computer-speak. All the better newspa-

pers were struggling, as if the news were no longer a priority or even a convenience. News was now a function of the mill called social media, as if it were the proletarian version of the Social Register. But what did he know? He was an old man living in a very old part of the world.

It was then that Ned Ayres liked to think he had been part of a golden age that was never to repeat itself in any recognizable form. That was the fact of the matter, and what Ned was trying to get down on paper, his memoir, was not as simple a chore as one might think. At the end of a day's reading and writing Ned found himself in a wilderness. These many years later he discovered that his stories were stale. They did not flourish on the page. His beautiful symphony had gone sour, the musicians weary after such a long haul. The newspaper business reminded him of his manor house, still handsome but no longer stately. The lawn was ragged. The third floor had long since been closed off, so late at night Ned no longer heard the soft midnight sounds of Edgar Allan Poe trying to put things right. Earl Bosenquet was long gone and replaced by a middle-aged woman from town who did not mind preparing a light dinner now and again. The anatomy of the house, its skin and bones and marrow, continued to break down, and to restore all of the parts to anything like what they had been — well, that was a fortune squandered. That was the man standing under a cold shower tearing up thousand-dollar bills and calling it ocean racing.

Commodore Ayres.

Ned Ayres was a popular figure in the village, whose inhabitants he found wildly eccentric, reminiscent of the disheveled newsrooms of his youth. The watermen especially spoke in a tongue so slurred and accented, seemingly composed of vowels alone, that he found it difficult to parse. Any outsider was obliged to listen carefully, and so it was fortunate that listening carefully was an old Ned habit. The weekly newspaper had folded long ago and a coffee shop had taken its place, patrons arriving with news of the fire on Bass Avenue or the break-in at the filling station — or was it the other way around, a break-in on Bass Avenue and a fire at the filling station? In the mornings when the weather was iffy Ned drove to the village and settled in at the coffee shop to keep abreast of things, and now and then there was real news, another teenager dead of an overdose, a teachers' strike imminent, tomorrow's rainstorm. His companions over coffee were the mayor and the police chief, both women in their seventies. The present was so discouraging that they talked mostly of the peaceable past, the Christmas parade and the school pageant. That very afternoon a carnival was setting up in the soccer field behind the school. They often recollected a fresh anecdote concerning Wilson's Fifty, the time the secretary of the navy fell off a horse. The afternoon old Wilson broke the ankle of the solicitor general with an errant croquet ball. How ya doin' up there, Ned? Things quiet at the Fifty? Ned said he was doing fine, though the other day Myrtle the cleaning lady came upon trespassers, nonthreatening trespassers who claimed they had lost their way. They gave Myrtle an uneasy feeling, a man and his son, city types wearing overcoats and fedora hats. They looked like bail bondsmen. Shifty characters, didn't know where in hell they were. But Myrtle was not one to be trifled with, so the trespassers went away.

Gets lonely, doesn't it? the mayor said.

I have my work, Ned said.

That's what you said when you came here, how many years ago now? "I have my work." We were pretty sure you couldn't stick it out. The Eastern Shore's not to everyone's taste. But you proved us wrong.

Takes time, Ned said.

We thought you'd miss the big city. Bright lights.

I did at first but not anymore.

You're an adaptable fellow, the mayor said.

They were standing on the sidewalk watching workmen assemble the Ferris wheel. Fanning out from the Ferris wheel were canvas lean-tos, spaces for food and drink and the various games on offer. Hit the bull's eye, win a kewpie doll. The workmen were taking their time, making frequent visits to the beer tent. The police chief shook her head.

She said, Accidents waiting to happen.

They're just boys, Ned said.

That's the trouble, the chief said.

We had carnivals in the little town I grew up in, Ned said. There was a girlie tent, so that usually meant a fistfight before things wrapped up. Hard cases from the next town over, Mill City. Everyone waiting for the fistfight, which usually ended in a draw. Always a few injuries. Our town tried to impose an admission fee for the hard cases from Mill City. Never worked. Or it didn't work to our advantage. The fistfight was part of the fun, I guess. The paper I worked for always had a page-one story on the fistfight. Above the fold, two photographs.

This one ends with fireworks, as you'll remember, the mayor said. In the old days they had an elephant. But the elephant died. Poor old thing, just keeled over. That was twenty years ago. You going, Ned?

I'm too old for carnivals, Ned said. All that standing around.

I'll buy you a beer, the chief said.

Was there trouble last year? I can't remember.

The chief shook her head. Rained like crazy. Damned deluge.

Ned said, Rain dampens high spirits.

Not always, the mayor said.

They stood quietly watching the Ferris wheel rise slowly, chair by chair. The chairs looked flimsy, as if a stiff wind could carry them away. Ned opened his mouth to say something, then didn't. The carnival was not his affair, and lately he had come to avoid crowds. Crowds gave him mild vertigo. He felt a lack of agility among strangers. Carnivals were fun, though, always something anticipated, like a fistfight or a child in distress. The idea of a leisurely beer had appeal. He thought he would go home to the manor house and have a beer. There was a six-pack in the fridge, Amstel. He would have a beer and a ham sandwich while he figured out where Uncle Ralph fit into the scheme of things. Uncle Ralph slipped into his mind unbidden and now his presence was palpable, his fact-free zone and his difficulties with his brother the judge. All his life Ned remembered the German soldiers, their comity and their gift-bearing, candy bars and chocolate bears, and soon enough they were gone, vanished into a French twilight. Uncle Ralph had created his own private war in which there were no casualties, always excluding himself. You had to admire Uncle Ralph's arrangements, a way to get through the day. Ned stepped back, away from the crowd. At dusk he would watch the fireworks from his Adirondack chair. He said goodbye to the mayor and the police chief, Paulette and Eloise, and strolled to his car. Ned looked back at the Ferris wheel. Work had ceased. There was a glitch and no one seemed to know what to do about it.

Ned Ayres drove slowly out of town, past the empty piers and the fish market. Someone waved and he waved back. Ned motored to the highway, turned left, and began the slow crawl to the manor house. The sun had begun its descent as the earth turned. Traffic thickened, everyone heading for the carnival. The Ferris wheel was visible in his rearview mirror. He passed the mayor's house and, a mile or so on, the Bosenquets'. He noticed thunderheads in the west; so there would be rain for the carnival. Then Ned turned into his brick driveway. A flight of blackbirds scrambled overhead. In only a few moments the manor house appeared through the trees. The sun disappeared behind a thunderhead. Ned wondered who would occupy it when he was gone. In his will he had deeded the house and its fifty acres to the town for a museum or whatever the town wanted. That was years ago. His lawyer tried to talk him out of it. The house was uninsurable owing to decay. A white elephant, the lawyer said. Who would want your house? The town won't take it. The town's broke. It's out of the way, Wilson's house. It's too big and it needs repair. You haven't kept it up properly, Ned. It's gone to seed. Now the land, that's something else. Someone with vision could make a fine property, ten or twelve houses for the Washington people who want a summer place. A gated community. That, I could sell. I could sell the hell out of it and you could leave the money to the library or the Boy Scouts. The high school needs a grown-up playing field with bleachers and two locker rooms. A big scoreboard. They'd call it Ned Ayres Field. Something to remember you by, Ned.

You never married, did you?

No, Ned said.

No living relatives?

None, Ned said.

Well, then, the lawyer said, and that was all he said.

I'll think on it, Ned said, but he didn't think on it. The lawyer died, and the idea died with him. Ned lost interest, what interest he had. He was now wholly occupied with his memoir and the recollections that went with it. The fragments, he called them.

• • •

Ned Ayres had begun with high enthusiasm for his new life, making what repairs he could and setting up a work schedule—one hour in the morning and two hours in the afternoon, bisected by lunch and a nap. He thought he could finish in two years, maybe three. There was no rush, and any deadline was his own deadline. He foresaw a long, loose glide path that ended in his library, an office so unlike his other offices. He thought of Poe's fragment and the Alma-Tadema. From the far corner of the library he watched the antique clock mark the minutes, a ding every quarter hour. For a time this annoyed him, but after a while he forgot about it. Everything depended on his memory and the reliability of his diaries and other papers. Of course Ned Ayres had difficulty in the beginning, his thoughts turning naturally to Herman and his apprenticeship in the correct presentation of news. In those days he lived in the moment without thoughts of tomorrow, entirely consumed by his line edits and two-sentence ledes, the first anchoring the second. He insisted that Gus Harding use two-sentence ledes, the mill that set things up for the grist. The lede was like a smart hat, the second thing the reader noticed. All this was the minutiae of news reporting but essential also. He thought of the minutiae as the stretcher-bearers of the campaign, skilled in triage. The triage came first. He remembered Gus Harding looking at him without comprehension. Ned was sympathetic. Sometimes you could take these strictures too far, make more of them than they were worth. But when one loved the business, insisted on its importance, well, a little exaggeration did no harm. Years ago Ned tried to spell out the idea to his father, who responded, Oh, for Chrissakes. But no one ever accused the judge of having the soul of a poet. Instead, he believed in his briefs. When Ned told him he had met William O. Douglas, Eric Ayres rolled his eyes: Douglas did not have a mind, he had a personality. The old man was baffled when Ned told him that a number of newsrooms around the country called the two-sentence lede the Ayres Lede. The Muncie paper did. The Indianapolis paper also, and others round and about.

Ned had not returned to Herman in years. What excitement there was he had mostly forgotten, and reasonably so. That was what you did with a used-up newspaper, forgot it along with yesterday's weather and the ball scores and the obits. Ned thought to place himself in that time, eighteen years old and so little had stuck; there were many lessons learned, but he had forgotten what they were except for the two-sentence lede. He did not begin a diary until years later when he had bought the green leather notebook with the Mark Cross logo, all but effaced over the years. Ned studied photographs to help him recall what downtown Herman looked like, the great swath of Benjamin Franklin Boulevard and the newspaper office next to the pharmacy, Grant Haberdashery down the street. He studied photographs to see what he looked like as a young man not out of his teens, six feet two inches tall, a tousled head of dark hair, unusually large eyes, capable hands, an untroubled smile, a squint following the smile. As a young man he had forged ahead willy-nilly. Falling upstairs, as they said. He was not born to the trade, but at the Herman *Press-Gazette* he had learned to read type upside down, made corrections faster than any of the regulars. But his memory, infallible for years, failed to find his boyhood self. He learned to live with that. In the high-vaulted library he pressed on, searching for the bits and pieces of a life back then, a snapshot of Elaine, another of Uncle Ralph, his mother in a fox stole, his father on the first tee of the golf club. Of course these were surface observations, as if his life were a procession of newspaper stories, "shorts," they were called. There was a Rosebud in there somewhere if he could find it. He did not have an up-to-date diary because there would have been so few facts to put in it. Often he turned to the computer, but the computer revealed little beyond years-old expense accounts and to-do lists, addresses and telephone numbers and income tax records and random notes deploring the high cost of newsprint. He was surprised one day to find a snapshot of Milo Passarel and Lana in the parking lot of the Alhambra.

Naturally there were no examples of his own work, the cutting and fitting, the word changes. Editing was as invisible as the work of a careful tailor. No one outside the newsroom could say, Nice edit, because readers never saw the edit. They saw the results of the edit. The edit was the live heart beating against the skin, essential yet concealed, crafted to endure. It was the mirror of the sea.

Ned Ayres persevered as the years accumulated. The manor house continued its slow, strained desuetude. The fields went to seed. The Adirondack chair, bleached white, was rarely occupied. Ned was slow afoot and rarely ventured beyond his house. The memoir became an avocation, like stamp collecting or billiards. His one certainty was that he would never complete it, and in time people stopped asking. In his off-hours he thought of a final resting place for his papers, such as they were. He had the idea to offer the archive to the Library of Congress, and when that went nowhere he considered a fine Maryland bonfire, invite his neighbors, serve champagne. It did occur to him to wipe the computer clean and send the contents to wherever they belonged in the ether. Someone told him that the word now was cloud. But at the last minute he could not bring himself to push the buttons, fate's temptation. Ned knew in his heart that was a kind of suicide, not so different from that wretch—what was his name? Grant. Born Kelly.